PROVIDENCE VANISHED

Adam

To a fellow fantasy enthusiast.
Enjoy.

Your Friend

[signature]

PROVIDENCE VANISHED

BOOK I
of
The Flames of Antioch

Adam Hoch

iUniverse, Inc.
New York Lincoln Shanghai

Providence Vanished

BOOK I of *The Flames of Antioch*

iUniverse, Inc.

For information address:
iUniverse, Inc.
2021 Pine Lake Road, Suite 100
Lincoln, NE 68512
www.iuniverse.com

Library of Congress Control Number: 2004096944

ISBN: 0-595-32729-X

Printed in the United States of America

CONTENTS

▼

Preface vii

Wakings 1

Unwanten Memorie 31

Taenarus 41

Bynethe the world 56

A Tour Sighte 73

Parting 96

Troublable Dreems 104

An Olden Rym 115

Biginne al newe 132

Author's Note 153

Endnotes 155

Preface

Providence Vanished is the first book in a series of seven called *The Flames of Antioch*. It is a hybrid of two genres, classical epic and modern fantasy, in both form (the journey of a larger-than-life person or ideal through trials, tribulations, and tests vs. the actions and events that occur in the changing of an age) and style (high epic poetry vs. prose). With that said, expect a unique blend of prose and poetry, theory and theology, and mystique and mythology in this epic tale.

Sections of *Providence Vanished* are written in Middle English, a language more eloquent in tongue than on paper. For your convenience the sections are brief, and included at the end of the book are the English translations.

So liven up and listen well…

Of changing age I seek to tell, As
writ in myth by bard divine inspired
or tangled lore from muse bemired, O thou
who watched the passage fly, now sing to me
of how and why ages alter recalling time...

WAKINGS[1]

Sarah and Malachai left the darkness of their one-room cottage and walked into the mild night air. They stopped at the top step of the porch and stood together, staring eastward into the ancient forest before them. Vibrant green underbrush surrounded the feet of the great maple trees that towered into the air, their branches swaying regally though there was no wind. The last rays of a departing sun fell upon the highest boughs as a golden hue, contrasting the darkness below, a darkness that meant more than an end to the day. This darkness began the end of an age.

The oracles appeared young, skin as soft and radiant as the coming moon's light, hair rich with color—Sarah's a light brown, Malachai's a darker—posture strong yet relaxed. The only thing that betrayed the oracles' age was their eyes; for they were white, marks of the race, and sparkled with knowledge of ages and legends past.

Both oracles wore silken garments. Sara's were green trimmed with gold, Malachai's purple and gold. A trace of wind stirred, ruffling the clothes. The colors shimmered, faded, dulled into bland blues and dirty whites. It was not the first time this had happened, nor would it be the last. The clothes were changing, as was the cottage.

The maple-wood beams of the old building were flawless and flecked with rich grains, never creaking with the changing of seasons or blowing of wind. From the cottage's northern side rose a brownstone chimney surrounded by wooden shingles that extended over the entire roof.

Though nothing stirred in the forest darkness, Sarah and Malachai remained where they were and listened to the swaying trees, listened for word of the rider.

Days came and went.

On the fifth night of their wait a cold wind drifted through the forest and across the small meadow, where the cottage huddled between the forest and the base of a large mountain. The wind brought a thick mist that swallowed the entire forest whole, numbing the trees. The old branches slowed their swaying, as if drugged. Dampness wrapped its icy fingers around the vigilant oracles.

Hungry, stiff, tired, and now cold they moved not but slightly. Malachai pulled his woolen blanket tight around his chest, his fine silk clothes gone, replaced by denim overalls that chaffed his increasingly sensitive skin. Sarah coughed, pulled her blanket tighter, and huddled against her husband.

On the seventh morning, rosy-fingered dawn appeared behind a veil of forest, fog, and cloud. Slowly, ever so slowly, darkness surrendered to dreary light. For the first time since the mist had descended, the forest spoke in hushed whispers. The branches swayed freely, the leaves rustled, lifted from the spell.

Deep in the forest a single leaf flew from a tree, fluttered downward through the boughs, and landed on the hard earth. A horse's hoof, cracked and bloody, landed next to it, then continued forward.

*   *   *   *

"He's here," Sarah cackled, breaking the long silence. She stepped away from her husband and disappeared into the cottage. The wallboards had begun warping and showed tinges of green where moss grew. The moss was most apparent at a section of roof near the chimney where a hole, no larger than Sarah's thumb, allowed cold air to seep into the house.

Sarah took two candles from a wicker basket beside the doorway and set them on the mantle of the fireplace. After cleaning out bits of melted wax from two wooden candlesticks, she fixed in the new candles and lit them. She then cleared away the half-burned wood from the fireplace and, in the middle, stacked new twigs and logs on top of dried bark. Sarah closed her eyes and focused. In seconds smoke poured from the wood, and, with a little puff, the thin wood flamed, quickly caught, and the fire spread.

Without missing a step, Sarah grabbed a cauldron and took it around the back of the cottage to the spring. She paused a moment to look into the deep well. Before, she would have seen the Book of Antioch deep in the water, beyond it a world of light and green leaves. Now the book was gone, the world beyond closed off. She knew in her heart it would be so, but had hoped otherwise—hoped that the book was where she and Malachai had cast it thousands of years ago. But now she knew for certain.

A lone tear escaped her eye and dropped into the pool, creating ripples that soon smoothed away. "It's not the end," she said, pulling back her sadness. "Only a change."

The sadness left completely at Sarah's will, and she went about her business as if it were a joy. She filled the cauldron with water from the spring, returned to the house, and hung the cauldron above the ever-strengthening flames before hobbling sprightly to the thick table. The hobble was new to her step, but she barely gave it a thought; the change had come.

Two wooden plates that once had been silver sat on the table. Greenish mold stretched over chunks of mutton and bread, supper that had been left seven days ago when the whisperings began and Sarah and Malachai were given a vision of the book. In the vision it was night and the oracles were standing at the spring, looking through the silvery water at the book. It was in the clutches of a boy, a boy named David.

Sarah smiled at the memory, which seemed as if it had happened eons ago. She smiled in sadness, which turned to remembrance, then curiosity and amusement. Chaos would return to this land because of a ten-year old boy.

"A ten-year old boy." Sarah cackled, and dumped the moldy food into a slop bucket.

After the plates were rinsed, dried, and stacked, Sarah turned to a set of shelves, which held dried herbs, spices, animal bones, and other items in jars and baskets. She took a few choice herbs and bones, and set them on the table along with a small square of tightly woven cloth. She took small, exact amounts of ingredient from their containers—four leaves of Witch Hazel, seven of Purslane, one small root of Curly Dock, a pinch of dried May Apple—and set them in the middle of the cloth. Once done, she gathered the ingredients inside the cloth and tied them in with a short piece of twine. This bundle she tossed into the cauldron.

*   *   *   *

The rider was no more than a shadow in fog, still distant from the cottage, when Sarah walked into the house. Malachai stretched his tired legs, gathered a knife and fresh maple branch, and sat on the porch steps. He whittled and whistled and watched as the shadow meandered through the great trunks, taking each step awkwardly and with great effort, following no path but the longest. Back and forth the shadow came, sometimes stopping, swaying, resting.

Sarah emerged from the cottage with a cauldron and went around back. When she returned ten minutes later, she set the cauldron on the porch, stood by Malachai, and thoughtfully looked into the forest.

"Tis true, Malachai," she said. "It's gone."

"I know, woman. I know." Malachai set the carving aside and clasped his wife's hand. "A sad day it is."

"Only if it sees us apart."

"The fates willing," Malachai said, "you an I'll see another age together."

"Twould be cruel any other way."

"We'll not know either way."

"Tis all the crueler," Sarah said. She delicately kissed Malachai's aging hand and disappeared into the cottage. Malachai returned to his carving, slowly forming the wood into its predestined shape.

As the day passed, the shadow neared, became discernable; gray shades transformed to definition and dull color. The rider was slumped on the back of his horse, arms and head dangling lifelessly across the animal's large neck. Mud, grime, and blood caked the rider's black cloak and boots. Fresh blood trickled from his head and ran down the horse's neck, as it strained forward weakly. Each step the animal took was clumsy. Drool and blood flowed from its mouth, ran down its flanks. Its mane was caked with mud and clumped together, on the verge of falling out.

Malachai nodded his head in reverent pity for the creature; the animal had fulfilled his last, most important errand on the wide green earth.

The horse entered the clearing, kicked a clump of dirt, and nearly toppled over before regaining balance. Malachai looked up from his carving but made no move to help. The creature staggered to the splintering wood of the porch and swayed in place, muscles quivering. The horse wheezed, spraying the ground with its lifeblood.

Malachai finally set the wood and knife on the porch floor and stood, his bones creaking loudly. He walked down the steps and waved a hand in front of the horse's eyes. The creature relaxed, its forced breath easing, pained eyes softening, trembling legs strengthening, allowing it to lie gently. Malachai gathered the rider from the steed's back and took him inside the cottage.

In the corner nearest the newly kindled fire was a bed of straw covered with a thin woolen blanket, upon which Malachai laid the rider. Sarah dipped some of the steaming broth from the cauldron into a wooden bowl and brought it to Malachai.

"It'll not build his strength, yet," she said. "It'll only keep him from dying."

"I know, woman." Malachai tipped the bowl to the rider's lips. "You'll have fresh marrow within the hour."

The rider coughed, sat up wide-eyed, and then relaxed, laid back down. His eyes closed and his body went limp, and Malachai drained the rest of the liquid into his mouth. The rider swallowed slowly.

"Thessaly," he said hoarsely, distantly. "I've com…"

"Shhh," Malachai interrupted. "Drink and sleep."

And the rider did.

✳   ✳   ✳   ✳

It was dark outside. Dark and cold. Perseus awoke to the smell of cooking meat, thick and greasy. The smell gave him hunger to accompany his pounding head and feverish body. He felt as if he had been trampled by a herd of antelope and left to rot in the desert sun—a sun that made him sweat as evenly as it made him shiver. He knew he was not in the desert, though he did not know where he was, or how he got here. It did not seem to matter at present. He was hungry, and the sweet aroma, the rich aroma, laden with exotic spices, was no more than an arm's length from him. And that's where his mind clung.

Slowly, Perseus opened his eyes and allowed them to adjust to the dim light. He was lying on the floor, his head rigid and staring up. A flickering of light, a fire, showed a mantle's stone to his left, and higher up a decaying roof. Stars shone through three large holes in the roof. One star in particular caught Perseus's eye, sparing him the aroma for a brief second. It was the jewel star—part of the Great Hunter. There was something wrong with it, something he could not quite comprehend…

Halfway through the thought, the smell of meat returned and his stomach rumbled. Perseus fought the exhaustion surrounding everything but the smell and tried to lift his head. A searing pain shot through his neck and imploded behind his eyes, causing him to scream and lie still. Stars flooded his vision, pushing the stone, ceiling, and sky into nothingness.

A few seconds later, just after Perseus's vision returned to normal, muffled footsteps came through an entryway and walked to the opposite side of the room. The footsteps paused, scuffed the floor, and walked over to Perseus. They belonged to a lean man wearing overalls and a dirty straw hat. His hair was brown but graying. His eyes were hidden by shadows, yet Perseus could see hard work heavily etched into the man's face. The man tipped a wooden bowl filled with broth to Perseus's mouth. He drank greedily, as if a hundred days had passed since his last draught, and then slept.

*   *   *   *

Light came through the open doorway, the lone window, and the five holes in the roof, yet the cottage still looked dreary. It was the light of dawn—a light of hope—yet it was cold. Perseus turned his head slowly. His neck was stiff and tender, but there was no pain. A great relief.

The fireplace was dead, the ashes gone. Slim memories of the aroma of cooking meat revisited Perseus, bringing with it a hunger that seemed impossible. His stomach felt an empty chasm.

Perseus pushed himself backward to the wall with unsteady arms. With difficulty he sat up, the woolen blanket falling off, and leaned against the wall for support. He pulled the blanket back across his exposed skin and pulled it tight. It was warmer, but only a little.

Across the room, in one corner, was a barrel; in the other corner, a cauldron. Both were separated by a table that was empty save for a wooden bowl. The wall adjacent to the one with the table was lined with shelves that held spoons, knives, bowls, water bladders, stone carvings, bones, cloth strips, and countless jars and baskets that were filled with dried herbs and spices Perseus could not identify.

The hunger strengthened, and brought with it a dry warmth. Perseus remembered the old man feeding him broth that made him sleep and forget the pain. He wished for more broth, but preferably some with meat and vegetables.

"Sire," Perseus cried weakly, and wondered at the rough sound of his voice. He cleared his scratchy throat and tried again. "Sire."

It came out louder, but quickly died in the silence. Perseus massaged his throat and waited for an answer, hoped the man would come. His hunger grew. His thoughts returned to the smell of cooking meat, moved to an older memory—the parting feast before his journey.

Pigs, turkeys, chickens, and cattle had been slain in sacrifice, in honour of Perseus, in homage to the gods that they might keep him safe. After the ritual, Perseus ate of the meat and other foods. There were potatoes of all kinds, corn, beans, beets, and other vegetables, each prepared several different ways. There were baskets of different breads and tables of pies, cakes, and candies. The wine flowed the night through as bards played tribute to journeys prior and to those yet to come. All this taunted Perseus as he sat on the straw bed, wrapped in a thin woolen blanket.

He cried out one last time, resolved to find food for himself if unanswered. But this time, before long, he heard a soft thud from outside the doorway followed by several creaks. Padded footsteps walked across the porch, bringing with them a form that stood in the doorway, tall and gaunt. The man was silhouetted against the morning backdrop, yet did not cast a shadow.

"Sarah," the man called out the door toward some unknown place. "Sarah, our boy's come round."

He wore the same straw hat and overalls as the man yesterday, yet this man's hair was fully gray, his face wrought with wrinkles, skin pale and covered in dark maroon spots. The man walked over to the bowl on the table, grabbed it, and brought it to Perseus.

"You're nearly finished," he said, kneeling down. "Only a couple more spoonfuls."

Perseus stared, his mouth wide and unbelieving. The old man's eyes were white, completely white. The old man smiled, his mouth emptied of all but a handful of teeth. He knew that Perseus had noticed.

"You're...you're the oracle of legend," Perseus stammered.

The old man nodded. "I'm one of em. But we'll talk bout that later. You won't sleep for more n' a couple hours."

Perseus took the bowl, keeping his eyes on the oracle, and drank the last of the draught. Within seconds, his head felt heavy, his eyes closed, and he fell into a deep slumber.

*   *   *   *

That night Perseus awoke ravenous. He was curled up on top of the blanket and straw mattress, and for the first time realized he was naked. A roaring fire burned in the fireplace; a cauldron hung just above. Flames licked the bottom of the pot, while steam escaped the top and exited through the chimney. Thick glubs popped from the brew, and an occasional drop of brown liquid flew over the cauldron's rim, landing in the fire.

An old woman was bent over the table, her back to Perseus, silvery hair tied in a loose ponytail. A long plain dress garnished her plump frame. Strings of an apron held the dress taut around her middle. She had been setting dishes around the table, but now was standing up straight, her head cocked slightly to the left.

"Awake, dearie?" she asked, and turned around. "Of course you are. And hungry, I suppose."

Her face was slightly wrinkled and showed kindness. But there was something hidden beneath, a glimmer of youth. As she neared Perseus though, and beckoned him to stand, he saw her eyes of liquid white and knew the ancient wisdom they held.

"Well, up with you. Ain't nothing wrong. Not now anyway."

She smiled warmly as she looked Perseus's naked body up and down. Perseus covered himself with the blanket, pulling it up to his chin.

"Embarrassed eh?" the woman said in her shrill, yet calming voice. Perseus flushed against his will. He relaxed and let the blanket fall down about his chest. The woman gave his body another casual glance before taking the cauldron off the fire. "I've seen worse," she said and laughed, lugging the full and blackened cauldron to the table. "Come on now. Don't be bashful."

Perseus stood gingerly, expecting sharp stabs in his chest and abdomen, expecting his bones to grind together as they had when he last mounted his horse, expecting to feel the relentless hours of pain he had missed while unconscious. But standing took surprisingly little effort. His muscles were stiff but not sore, his ribs tender but not broken. Perseus wrapped the blanket around his waist and twisted his torso, stretching, hoping the pain would not return.

He was surprised at how good it felt to stretch, how enlivening and invigorating. It was as if the battles and injuries in Argolis never took place. Even the aches in his shoulder and hip, unyielding pains from childhood, were gone. It was as if the past three years of hardship were a memory, a dream, a conclave of distant adventures that were not his own.

Perseus almost believed it was so. He wanted to believe it was so. But it wasn't. His scars spoke of the truth. Many thin scars, two and three fingers long, were sewn into his skin, front and back. Stab wounds. Fatal stab wounds to their makers. How many people had he slain, lured in close enough to run through? How many times had he felt the cold point of steel pierce his skin, a minor blow, in order that he could deliver a fatal one? Perseus could not remember.

There were three larger scars, as thin as the smaller ones, but thrice and four times as long. Many times, countless times in Argolis, he had been a hair's breadth from a fatal swing. Three times he had been closer. One scar crossed above his left breast, ashen against otherwise healthy skin. One sluiced diagonally downward on his left side, the same ivory paleness as the first. The last of these scars traveled just beneath his naval; there the skin was red and bloated. He ran a finger across the raised flesh and felt the tenderness.

"Almost killed you," the old woman said gravely, touching an old finger to the scar. Perseus cringed at the burning tingle that settled where the crooked finger had been. "Still tender, yes." The old woman lowered her finger slowly, and clasped Perseus's wrist with an unnaturally strong grip. "It almost killed ye," she said again, staring dangerously into Perseus's eyes. "But it didn't. Remember that, young one, remember."

The woman led Perseus to the table alongside the far wall. A small candle set in a plainly carved holder bathed the table in a soft glow, catching the contours of the wooden dinnerware at odd slants. The woman left Perseus in the chair at the head of the table, filled a bowl with a brown stew from the cauldron, and set it before Perseus. Chunks of meat, carrots, leaks, potatoes, and other, foreign ingredients floated before his eyes, sang to his stomach a sweet and loving lullaby.

"Go on," the woman said. "Have at it."

Dizzy with hunger, Perseus inhaled the stew, finishing the first bowl just as the woman put three large loaves of fresh bread, a bowl full of creamy butter, a wheel of cheese, and a cup of water on the table. Perseus cut a large chunk of cheese and half a loaf of bread as the woman filled his bowl.

"That's it," the woman said, setting the bowl down. "Eat up. It's been long since you've tasted food, I think. Eat up, now. You'll be hungry for a while yet."

Five bowls of stew, two and a half loaves of bread, the entire wheel of cheese, and seven glasses of water were gone before Perseus's stomach was contented. The woman had all the while been filling Perseus's bowl and cup in addition to cleaning the small cottage. When Perseus had finished, the woman was tending the fire and humming softly. He listened to the beautiful tune for a moment before pushing back his chair, kneeling on the ground, and bowing his head.

"Madam," he said in the olde tongue, "yow and yourne haf doon me a kind servyse. I am blessed by youre sanctity and grace, and wol paye yow for the compassioun however I myght."[2]

The woman turned around, laughing. "Tis a long time since I heard the speech of old, young one. Pleasant, but not wanted."

"But yow art an oracle,"[3] Perseus said.

"Right you are, dearie. Now stop this foolishness and get off yer knees."

"As you wish," Perseus said, feeling slightly abashed. He rose and sat in the chair. The woman went back to tending the fire, placing thin sticks atop the fiery coals. "My name is Pe—"

"I know who you are," the woman said, cutting him off, delicately placing another stick. "You are the rider."

With the woman's words came a deep and calming warmth, causing Perseus alarm. The last time he felt like this, he was almost lost to the world, transformed by a tree nymph. That memory seemed a lifetime ago, distant beyond recall, until the old woman spoke—*you are the rider.*

Perseus was overcome with warmth, the sweet feeling of death; it was lulling him to sleep, to death. He tried to stand up, wanted to find his sword, his clothes; he wanted to rush out of the cottage, jump on Nemesis, and be off ere the sleep could take hold. Nemesis. Where was Nemesis?

"Woman," he said gruffly, groggily, unable to move. "What have you done with my horse?"

"He is no more," the woman said, words melting into one another, softening and dipping. "His last breath to spare yours."

Perseus nodded as if he remembered. And indeed he did remember, if remembering comes in the form of a dream. But the dream had been real. Nemesis's strong flanks weakening, stumbling, halting. The horse's wheeze, sick and dying, beneath Perseus's broken body. Calmness descending through air, gently stopping. The feel of the end. Was it a dream? He didn't know. He couldn't move. His arms and legs lay limp, traitors to his will.

"What…are you doing to me?" he managed defiantly, one last shred of dignity poured into the world, his head light and wispy, drooping back, eyes heavy, sinking.

"You have nothing to fear from me, young one. Me or my husband."

Perseus nodded in agreement, believing the woman. It was her words, their sensual texture and silky feel that helped him believe. A trick of an oracle, perhaps. Or the truth. He was helpless to tell which. It didn't matter.

He watched the woman through a gray fog that continually blackened. From a basket, the woman took out thin, green sticks and wove them together, bending and forming their slender bodies. She resumed humming, head slumping, eyes closing darker, wanting to stay awake.

"I've come from…" Perseus said, hoping. But the words drugged him deeper.

"You've come from the east," the woman finished, eyes closed, dark. "I know. We've been waiting."

*   *   *   *

"…shouldn't have put him to sleep," Perseus heard the old man say kindly. It was the first thing that cohered as reality, allowing Perseus to understand he was awake. Although he had heard other words first, they had blurred with the wild dreams he had been having; their true meaning remained lost in strange thoughts. These words though, he understood, and knew the man was talking about him.

"I'll do what I please," the woman said defensively.

"As always, woman. As always." The old man deliberately turned his back to her and hung his straw hat on a peg beside the door. In the low light, Perseus saw a head of silver hair surrounding a large bald spot.

"Besides, it was only for a few moments, so I could finish."

"Finish what?" Perseus asked shortly, fully awake, hands flexing, legs moving at will.

"You'll see in a moment," the woman said, and flashed him a kindly smile. She took a seat on the bench beside the long end of the table. The old man sat next to her. Both of their faces looked haggard and older than they had at last sight. Smudges of dirt lay upon the old man's forehead and overalls; it also covered his hands and filled the undersides of his rough fingernails. "Now then, dearie, we can talk if you like."

"Very well then," Perseus said, "Sire, Mad—"

"Sire?" the old man said incredulously, cutting Perseus off. "No, no, my dear boy. I am Malachai. And this is Sarah."

"But you are oracles."

"Sharp one isn't he?" Sarah said dryly.

"I'll not speak to you as commoners."

"Won't speak to us as commoners?" Malachai laughed. "Imagine that. Telling *us* he won't speak to us as commoners. And what's wrong with commoners?"

"That's not what I meant," Perseus said. "You deserve more respect." The two stared at him curiously with slim smiles. "You're oracles," Perseus added, as if it should explain everything.

"Oracles, yes. But we much prefer if you call us Malachai and Sarah."

"Very well then," Perseus said shortly, and then took a breath. "Malachai, Sarah, I am Perseus, son of Telemachus. Though I do not know where I am, I have come from Thessaly, sent by my father in search of an oracle. I am grateful, and humble, to have found the oracles of legend. The greatest of your kind. For your hospitality you shall be repaid. But by your leave, I also seek your wisdom.

"Three years I've been traveling the land, yet strangeness has come of late. The journey began after the birth of the first foal, and all was well until I came to Delphi. There I expected my journey to end. But instead it had just begun. I found the city in ruin. Where once a grand temple stood was only broken stone, laying waste in the heat of day. As was the fountain of Kassotis."

Perseus paused, emphasizing the destruction of the fountain and the temple of an oracle. He searched the old faces for signs of anger at the destruction. He searched the old faces for signs of disbelief or surprise. Yet, he saw no emotion other than slim amusement on the oracle's faces. Bewildered, he waited for a different reaction. A raise of an eyebrow. Shifting eyes. He let the silence grow sure that something would happen, yet no change overcame the oracle's smirks. There was no choice but for Perseus to continue the tale.

"Under the temple ruins I took relief from the sun," Perseus said, almost sounding confused. "There I napped and drank the las—"

"We know the world is changing," Malachai finally interrupted, "and are not surprised by what you speak. However, we also do not have time to hear more of your journey. The past is not an oracle's business. You came here in search of answers about the future, yes?"

"Yes," Perseus said. "About Thessaly and the threat of war from Phrygia."

"Poor boy," Sarah said, patting Perseus's hand. "That war never happened."

"No, but it may soon," Perseus said.

Sarah smiled sadly, tenderly. "Listen closely, for this will not be easy to understand. That war never happened. A great battle has taken place in its stead, a battle waged on Thessalian ground between forces you cannot yet comprehend. The battle has been over for more than a year, now, yet the war wages on."

"A year! What war? How can that be?"

"The world has changed much since you left," Malachai said.

"Time is not what it once was," Sarah added. "You have not been traveling for three years, but over twenty."

"Twenty years?" Perseus asked.

"Yes, twenty," Sarah said.

"How can that be?"

"The Book of Antioch has been found," Sarah said simply.

"The Book of Antioch," Perseus said. "It can't."

"It has."

"It can't. The book is nothing more than legend."

"It is legend, true," Malachai said. "But it is also truth. And it has been found."

Perseus sat for a moment in thought. He knew *of* the Book, but he knew very little *about* the Book. What he did know came from old riddles, myth, and legend told to him by his father. There were also the ancient parchments he had seen in Byblis that mentioned the book; but even that information was little if any.

"You have heard much about the book," Malachai continued. "Perhaps as much as any mortal knows these days. But you are far ignorant to its importance. I can see it in your thoughts. Shall I tell you the story, the true story?"

"Go on," Perseus said, and nodded.

"The book was once kept by the Moirai, who were guarded tirelessly by an order of priests."

"Guarded," Perseus said. "But why?" He had read part of this myth in the Tower of Byblis. It told of the Moirai and the priests who guarded the book. But the myth also said the book was nothing more than the ancient's wisdom, which could not surpass the wisdom of this age. Hardly the sort of thing to be guarded.

Malachai laughed. His white eyes swirled, held Perseus captive, quieted his questions.

"You're right, young one. I have not started back far enough. The Book of Antioch is an old artifact. Older than the world itself it's said. It does not just tell of the future. It tells of the past and the present as well. The book *is* the trinity of time. It has been sought by many people who wish for great power. For the person who rules the book can rewrite time as they please.

"The book was kept in the center of a palace in a room with the Moirai. The corridors leading thus were said to be long and winding. So much so that the priests were the only persons who knew their design. And along these corridors were said to be gateways that were kept by ancient spells and spirits. And still, the palace itself was said to be hidden with enchantments. All these securities set up to guard the book from the greedy hands of men. But all these securities were for naught.

"The book was stolen from the palace in the dead of night. Eight of the nine priests were found dead, decapitated. The Moirai and ninth priest were gone. In the time that followed, although no one knows how long it was, the world was ravaged by fire; the one who had stolen the book was rewriting it."

Malachai fell silent and let Perseus ponder his words. Perseus struggled to remember what he had read many years ago in the dingy basement of the Tower of Byblis. In all of the ancient parchments there was nothing of the rewriting of time. The parchments told that many sought the book because it was said to hold the wisdom that had been lost in the many fires, quakes, and other great disasters of history. Not because one could rewrite history.

"The thief surely didn't write the world into ruin," Perseus finally said.

"True enough," Sarah said. "But when one word is changed in the book, all others change with it. The book undergoes a metamorphosis within itself, until it is again in harmony. The tearing of a world is what caused the ruin."

"Chaos took the world from within," Malachai continued, "burning it from the inside out. The world was thrown into disorder while the book was missing. None save the oracles, the true oracles, had the power to set things right."

"It took thirteen of us," Sarah said, "to track the book down and return its contents to the original. Since then, the book was hidden and guarded."

"When the oracles returned the book to its former," Perseus said, "the world would have returned to its former as well…if what you are telling me is true."

"Wrong," Malachai said. "The book returned to harmony. It did not return to the same harmony. Many civilizations in the world were buried, lost for all time. And with them, went their knowledge. Your race became a fledgling race again. It was many hundreds of years before man learned language, and another couple hundred before the arts were born from the muses. But once that happened, bards were given inspiration. They were told of the book, and the story grew from word of mouth. The legend was passed down, changing with the teller, tales spinning true and false about origin and myth, growing and diminishing, until the story became just that: a story, true meaning lost to the wind. But I assure you, the book is real, and it has been found."

"It must be retrieved and hidden," Sarah said. "Lest it fall into the wrong hands."

Perseus took a deep breath. What the oracles were telling him was that the book was a true legend preceding all time, that it had been stolen millenniums ago, sending the world into chaos, that it had been recovered, and that now it had been found again. Every word was surreal, yet every word explained much: the chaos in Delphi and Delos. Then again in Argolis.

"Why tell me?" Perseus asked.

"You are the rider from the east," Sarah said. "It is you who are destined to retrieve the book."

"But yow art the oracles." Perseus said. "Is it not your burden?"

Malachai and Sarah smiled sadly. With a sigh, Malachai spoke. "When the book was taken from the Moirai and rewritten, our lot changed in this world."

"It cannot be so," Perseus said.

"It is the way things are," Malachai said. "It was the will of the fates, as it was their will that a ten year old boy should stumble on the ancient book."

"A ten year old boy?" Perseus asked.

"Yes," Sarah said and stood. "A boy named David. Come. I must show you this event, for it is most important to your task." She drew Perseus to the hearth and had him kneel before the fire. His attention was drawn into the glowing coals, entranced by the soft heat that bathed his face. She took a small orb, woven from the inner flesh of infant twigs, from the mantle and threw it into the fire. "Look into the orb, young one, and you shall see."

The orb floated on a cushion of air; the small woven twigs smoldered; the smoke caught in the center of the ball and swirled. In less than a minute, the orb was filled with light smoke that spun, little tendrils now reaching through the rough weave, wafting toward Perseus, seeking out his face.

Some caressed his eyes, bringing forth the vision of a young boy standing on the side of a hill next to a large yellow school bus; he was looking east. Other tendrils sought his ears, bringing with them a faint rumbling sound akin to thunder, but constant and heavier. Smoke swept into Perseus's nose, bringing faint smells of rancid tar, fumes. But underneath that smell was crispness, cleanness, coldness. It would soon be winter.

*   *   *   *

Although he had only stepped off the school bus a few seconds ago, David Trexler's nose was already chilled in the late fall air. It had been a bad day at school; stupid Denny with his stupid friends had threatened to beat him up again, and in gym class, Joey booger-brains told Melissa Harpinger that David liked her—even though he didn't (not that much at least). And that wasn't all that happened in David's day that made it the worst day in history. But everything about the fifth grade left his mind as he looked east.

Underneath the cloud-blanketed sky, through a narrow band of space in the trees, David's eyes were drawn to Thaeron. The mountain sat quietly and undisturbed—except for the lights. They were dark, as black as night, yet they were lights, and stood out amidst the deep color of the mountain, glowing with a gloomy charm.

The black glow seeped into David's head, washed over his thoughts. The lights were speaking to him, whispering in the strange tongue that first came at the silvery pool. No matter how hard David tried, though, he couldn't understand what the voices were saying. To understand he needed to go to Thaeron, to the lights—that he was sure of. They were calling to him.

Vaguely aware of his best friend's presence, David took a few steps away from the bus, allowing Billy enough room to jump to the ground. The bus let out a loud hiss and grumbled away, leaving the two alone in David's front yard.

David absently wiped a string of snot from his nose as he watched the lights, heard the voices, thought of the book—the strange little book he'd found last week.

He had been playing in the woods, searching the ground for a twisted walking stick. Underneath the sparse brown and orange canopy, fallen leaves, branches, and jagged rocks had offered themselves to David as an adventurous landscape. And David had pretended he was in a land of danger, skirting the obstacles with care. He had whistled as he trudged, as he wandered, unaware of where he was going, not caring. He often did this when Billy couldn't come over—so often that he thought he knew every inch of the forest. The day he found the book, however, a day not yet a week removed, he had learned differently. On that day as he wandered, lost in thought, he came upon a place untouched by the seasons.

Grass, green and lush, sprung from the ground and surrounded powerful trees—stout trunks a rich brown, leaves as green as emeralds. David stood at the edge of the grass, afraid yet strangely comforted. He tentatively took a step forward into this haven. Immediately the air changed, became mild and sweet, smelling faintly of springtime flowers. David took off his jacket and looked around, unaware that he was still walking; his body seemed to float forward.

His eyes were drawn to a glimmer in the distance—light, perhaps reflecting off of a couple of quarters or a pearl necklace, something his mother would like. But what David found was a pool, limpid and silvery, shaded from the warming sun, whither no shepherd, nor his flock, nor bird, beast, or fowl had come; its radiance untouched by falling branches and leaves.

David bent down, charmed by the quiet pool and drank of his reflection, gazed into his eyes. Spellbound, he watched the boy, motionless as a marble statue, cheeks of ivory, red where a faint blush hit them. David reached out toward the figure, hand floating above the surface, when he saw the book on the pool's bottom, no more than an arm's length away.

His hand lingered but a moment before sinking into the icy coolness. That was when the whispers came, filling his mind with unintelligible words and ramblings, which caught his ear with a silken tongue. They felt good, though they were strange. David wanted to hear more; he wanted the book, and so sank his arm deeper, up to the elbow.

The book was still out of reach, the whispers, not louder, but stronger. David's shoulder broke the silvery surface, followed by his head, then body. Still the book was not within his grasp. He plunged into the abyss, swam further, downwards with all his tiny might, toward the book at the bottom of the pool.

It seemed an eternity till he felt a roughness beneath his fingers, a stone stuck in mud. David opened his eyes, swam further, finally reached the foreign book, and clasped it with his tiny hands.

A surge swept through his body, livening his senses. His lungs felt afire, desperate for air; his mouth tasted the cool sweetness of the water, and beyond the book David could see more than just the bottom of a pool. Beyond the book was stone, fitted in a small circle, a well. And beyond the stone was darkness, speckled with the golden dust of stars, faint and bright, twinkling from beyond a powerful veil. And then the stars were blotted out, replaced by silhouetted bodies.

Bethmar, yong sire[4], the voices whispered stronger, and through the silhouettes David saw four eyes, white-hot as the sun, searing, penetrating, warning. *Bethmar.*

As he clasped the book, he felt himself being pulled downward, toward the menacing eyes. He fought the current and his desperate desire to breathe, and swam upward, toward the murky light he knew as his own, toward the untouched pool in the green forest refuge.

Gasping, David broke the surface and clung to the pool's edge, the whispers fading. After a moment of panting he hauled the book from the water and slowly pushed it into the grass before pulling himself onto the bank. David sat in the grass, staring in amazement, the whispers gone. He was dry. And the book, the book was as dry as if it had never touched the pool.

The cover was a deep black, blacker than nothingness, yet it still shimmered brighter than the strange golden lettering on the cover.

$$\bar{\sigma}\text{\textbackslash}\text{'}\text{\textturnk}\text{\textcurrency}\ \Pi\text{\textrevsigma}\text{\textasciitilde}\ \text{\textlambda}\ \text{\textpi}\text{\textrevsigma}\text{\textrevsigma}\times\times\text{\textpi}\text{'}\text{\textgamma}\times\times\bar{\sigma}\text{\textcent}\text{-}\text{\textrevsigma}$$
$$\text{\textdagger}\text{\textdagger}\text{\textpi}\text{\textlambda}\text{\textbackslash}\text{\textrevsigma}\text{\textpi}\text{''}\text{\textcent}\times\bar{\sigma}\text{\textcent}\ \text{\textslash}\text{\textrevsigma}\ \text{\textsection}\ \text{\textrevsigma}\text{\textcent}\bar{\sigma}\text{\textdagger}\text{\textrevsigma}\text{\textlambda}\text{\textit{f}}\text{'}\Pi\text{\textrevsigma}\text{\textasciitilde}$$

David tried to lift the small volume to his lap, but couldn't. It looked no bigger than the Bible on his bed stand, the one his parents had given him, and it was certainly thinner, but it was heavy. Again, David struggled to lift the book, and succeeded in dragging it three inches. After a longer struggle, he finally had the book in his lap.

David shook off the memory and came back to the present, to Billy. He pointed at Thaeron, at the lights, directing Billy's eyes where they needed to go. "There's two of 'em," he said. "It's a sign Billy. I know it."

Billy strained his eyes and leaned forward. He couldn't see the lights. Hell, he could barely see the mountain with his poor eyesight. Past the trees that lined the road, the scene was a haze of yellows, reds, oranges, and browns. But then, suddenly, a sliver of glowing black appeared in the haze, just as David said it would.

"I see one," Billy said. Another sliver of strange blackness came into focus next to the first. "I see them," he corrected.

"Billy, it's the legend."

"The what?"

"The legend of Thaeron. There's treasure up there."

"Treasure," Billy repeated, continuing to stare. The lights, which minutes before seemed distant, now appeared to be the only things there. No colored leaves or trees; there wasn't even a mountain anymore. There were just the lights. "Wow. Treasure? Like gold and…and…and other stuff?"

"Yeah," David agreed. "We have to go to the mountain, Billy. We have to go soon."

"Go?" Billy asked nervously.

"Yes—there's gold."

"I don't know, David."

"Billy, this is big. It's bigger than big. Think about everything you can do with that money. You can buy all the Star Crunches in the world. The Nintendo you wanted…Mega Man, Super Mario Brothers, all the games Nintendo ever made. Just think Billy, think. You'll be rich. Forever. Maybe you can even move into a house. Maybe *I* can move into a house—a real house."

"A real house?" Billy said. "And clothes too. I can buy a pair of jeans. Maybe then people won't make fun of…"

His voice trailed off as he picked at the green sweat suit he was wearing. A pair of jeans would be nice. And maybe he could buy mom the couch she wanted. And after all that, there might even be money to buy some Star Crunches. A year's worth. No, two year's worth. Maybe even enough for a lifetime supply.

"Okay," Billy said hesitantly. His eyes came up to meet David's. "But why can't we wait for your mom to come home. She could drive us there. It wouldn't take as long. And…and then we wouldn't have to walk."

"That's not the way things are done," David said. "The death angel lives up there. And any bit of noise 'll wake im. We gotta walk. It's the only way."

"David," Billy began, and then caught sight of his friend's face. It looked different—possessed. Billy swallowed, thinking he didn't want to know the answer, but continued. "What's the legend of Thaeron?"

"It's the book," David mumbled, almost to himself, then spoke louder. "It's about…it's about Florida and fishing and jeans and Meliss—" David cut his words off, stayed quiet for a long moment, then said "it's about life," in no more than a whisper.

Without another word, not giving Billy any clue as to what the legend was, David walked across the small lawn, toward his trailer, and continued up the worn steps into the living room.

The air inside was thick and heavily laden with the stagnant smell of cigarette smoke. The single window next to the door was covered with blinds, allowing a small amount of light to filter around the edges. David flipped a switch on the wall, turning on the lamp across the room.

The light revealed a rectangular room with dark wooden paneling. It was furnished with an old yellow couch and chair, a scuffed up coffee table, and a twenty-six inch television. Above the television hung a faded painting of Jesus. To the right, the room opened into an adjoining kitchen. To the left, a thin, dark corridor led to the bedrooms and bathroom.

David fixated on the picture of Jesus. Long straight brown hair that was parted in the middle hung behind his robe-adorned shoulders. A trim brown beard surrounded a slim smile. The picture would have been nice had it not been for the man's eyes. To David they looked diseased, telling the story of a man that would hurt and then love, abuse and then embrace, save a life only to kill it. He shuddered and looked away; he'd had enough scrutiny for the moment. He took off his backpack and threw it on the couch.

"Can you empty that for me?" he asked Billy, and headed into the kitchen.

"Sure."

Billy closed the front door and sat on the couch. His eyes surveyed the room before inevitably wandering to the television and the small black box that sat next to it—the small black box that went up to the mini satellite dish on top of David's trailer. The dish was infinitely better than Billy's antenna, which brought in just over four channels.

Billy searched for the remote on the coffee table and in the cushions before noticing the gray plastic poking out from underneath the couch. He picked up the remote, hit the power button, and flipped to channel 318 to find his favorite show: *Rugrats*. This taken care of, he picked up David's backpack and absently emptied it of the loose papers, notebooks, and textbook.

A few seconds later, David was at the couch, holding four cans of Sprite, what looked like a pack of lunchmeat, a small pack of matches, and a box of Star Crunches—an *entire* box of Star Crunches. Billy licked his lips.

"David?" he asked, momentarily forgetting the television. "Can I have a Star Crunch?"

"Of course," David said, or Billy thought he had said.

All Billy really knew was that there was an entire box of Star Crunches in front of him, and that David was opening it slowly. Super slowly, in fact—slower than it took for the sun to travel across the entire sky. Billy could have had a thousand Star Crunch boxes open in the amount of time it was taking.

Finally one of the plastic covered snacks was slipped into his hand. And soon it was in his mouth, his taste buds melting along with the chocolaty, rice-krispity, caramel goodness. It had been at least a week since his last Star Crunch, and this one was better than he remembered. It was so good that he hadn't noticed David put the food and matches into the empty backpack before slipping off down the hallway.

David walked twenty paces, past two small bedrooms and one small bathroom, to the closet at the end of the hall. After turning on the closet light, he lay down and wiggled his body underneath the bottom shelf. His hand reached for the wooden paneling at the back and, finding it, his fingers ran along the rough surface. His index finger slipped through a small hole and with a gentle tug the trap door opened upwards, allowing enough room for David's hand to slide underneath, where he had stored the book.

When he clasped the rough cover, the voices whispered, sadly, sweetly, as if an angel were weeping. It was comforting to David to hear the voices, and he had often snuck down to the closet while his parents slept.

Bethmar the drakamor, the voices always whispered. *Bethm—*

The whispers cut off suddenly and abruptly, as if they had been severed with a knife. In the same instant, the trap door slammed downward, pinning David's hand between itself and the book. Pain seared through David's knuckles, ran up his arm and throughout his body.

Stifling a cry, he struggled against the trap door, which felt as if it was being pushed downward with ungodly force. Quiet tears spilled from his eyes until finally the door eased for a moment, a split second, allowing David to pull his hand and the book out from underneath the shelf.

…kamor, the voices whispered distantly, before disappearing completely, giving way to something else. Not whispers, but a feeling. A feeling that was greasy, that felt like oil spilling across David's thoughts. He ignored the feeling as best he could and pulled the book onto his lap with ease; it was now no heavier than a cushion of air.

It had taken him hours to drag the book away from the silvery pool, yet he had done it with careful diligence. With each inch he moved the book, the moving seemed to become easier, the book lighter. By the time he was at the edge of the strange grass the sun was on the horizon, but David could actually pick up the book. It took a mighty effort to carry at first, and David had to stop and rest many times, but the load lightened as he distanced himself from the pool till it almost seemed to carry him.

David again placed the book in his lap and looked at the shiny black cover and golden lettering. In the dim light of the hallway he flipped through the pages. They were full of strange marks and words, pictures and emptiness, symbols and riddles, all of which he couldn't understand. But on the last two pages there were words scrawled in English, most of which he could read, some of which were too faint or too smudged to read. But three words stuck out at the top of the second to last page—three words that left little streams of drool forming in David's mouth—*Thaeron, lights, gold.*

Absently wiping his nose, David turned the page. It was the final page. Fragments of words, a poem, danced in front of his eyes.

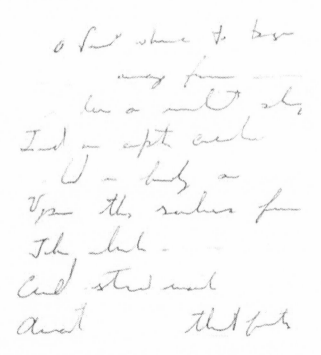

David thought for a minute before setting the book on the ground. He stood up and searched the closet shelves for the things he and Billy would need. Two minutes of rummaging produced three pennies, a bottle of hand soap, a roll of craft wire, and a small pocketknife. Each item was carefully placed on the book before David walked into the bathroom and opened the medicine cabinet. The creams, salves, ointments, and pill bottles went unnoticed. It was the crystal bottle on the top shelf—the one with the elegant lettering—that held David's attention.

For a moment, just one moment, he considered leaving without the bottle. But the potion inside was important, and that was that. There were things, evil things out there that needed to be guarded against. And besides, he could buy his mom a new bottle when he and Billy came back. Their pockets would be swimming with jewels and gold and fame. He could buy her a million new bottles of perfume.

It was settled; David grabbed the bottle and added it to the other gear. Cradling the supplies in his scrawny arms, he walked to the living room.

"What's all that?" Billy asked.

"Stuff for the trip. Can you give me a hand?"

Billy turned off the television and saw the book. Without thinking he reached for it. It was the most beautiful thing in the world and he didn't want to take his eyes off of it. He wanted to open it and read it and…and…touch it. But before Billy could feel the cover, David plunged the book into the bag, and the urge weakened. Billy wanted to tell David that the book didn't belong there; it belonged in the light, where he could look at it.

"David?" he asked hesitantly, and picked up the pennies. "What was that…that book?"

"It's the legend," David said. Billy put the pennies into the bag, and David clipped the straps shut.

"Can I…" Billy swallowed. He wanted to touch it, but something didn't feel right. Or rather, it felt too right. Just like the time he thought he was getting a bike for Christmas and hadn't. Billy watched anxiously as David shouldered the book bag, and surveyed the cluttered room. "Never mind," he finally said.

"Ready to go then?" David tugged his wool hat over his ears, walked to the door, and opened it.

"Wait," Billy said.

David stopped and turned, but Billy could only stare at his friend. There were no words to express the queerness he felt. What if they ran into some kind of monster? Or got lost? Or hungry? Billy thought of words, words to start a coherent sentence, and then lost them. He wanted to tell David about the bike, though David already knew that story.

No matter how hard he tried, he couldn't think of anything that would change David's mind. At last, one thing entered his mind. It was the only thing to enter his mind that made any sense. "I have to be back by dark."

"Sure, dark," David said nonchalantly. "Of course." He turned around and headed down the wooden stairs. Billy followed. "Dark," David repeated under his breath.

The cloud-filtered light cast eeriness across the land, causing shadows to seem no more than a lighter shade of black. The two walked across the lawn and turned right at the road, heading down Donaldson Hill. They stayed next to the shoulderless road, dried leaves crunching beneath their feet, heading toward Thaeron.

The front lawn was left behind, replaced on either side by forest—naked trees with moss growing at their bases, fallen branches straddling leaf-covered mud puddles, rocks, and patches of dried tall grass, still in the afternoon quiet.

Crunch, crunch, crunch went David's feet on the thin layer of leaves. Crutch, crutch, crutch went Billy's behind him. But that was it, no more sound from the woods. There should have been squirrels hopping along, playing a game of diaper tag or smear the queer or whatever game they liked to play. But there were none.

Crunch, crutch. Crunch, Crutch.

There should have been quail or maybe even a wild turkey hiding in the patch of tall grass, searching the ground for grasshoppers and worms. They would have taken off at the crunching leaves or, at the least, gobbled in fright. But none took off and none gobbled; there were none.

Crunch. Crutch.

There should have been a car zooming down the country road, music booming from the trunk, on its way to somewhere important; even the sound of cars from the nearby Fairfield road should have been audible—little swishes as they passed by Donaldson Hill. But there were none.

A slight breeze stirred, sending a round of dead leaves to wander through the forest.

Crunch.

Something was caressing David's hair. He scratched at it absently. The caressing increased, seeped into his scalp, deeper and deeper. It began to whisper, causing David to squirm. He tried to push it from his mind.

However, the presence grew stronger with each step, clearer in his mind, softer in his thoughts, inviting him in for a drink—or perhaps a snack. It was the same something he felt when the whispers had stopped, only now it was calling from the woods, there—to his right—no more than a glimmer through the trees. David looked and saw nothing, thought he saw nothing, wished he saw nothing. But a glimmer there was.

Deep within the forest, hidden behind giant oak and elm trees, soft light hung thick, causing the glimmer to emerge before young David's eyes. It captivated him, sang to him the sweet lullaby his mother used to sing, that he often whistled while walking in the woods—*wish that I was in the land of cotton*—called to David, to Billy, to come, come home.

David heard Billy's mind, saw Billy's thoughts. Billy scared and trying to fight the voice, the lullaby soothing and caressing, gentle as a summer's breeze. Billy trying to speak, to scream, to whisper, to anything; but he couldn't. He, they, could only listen and come home.

Come home the voice sang—*look away, look away, look away, Dixie land.*

It was an old man singing; it was lonely, David thought—no, he knew it was lonely. Lonely and alone. David knew it was an old man as Billy knew he was harmless and tired. It had drink and snack, Sprite and Star Crunches—all the boys could eat. All the boys could drink. It was harmless and lonely, just wanting some company and nothing more.

Crunch—crunch—crunch.

David was walking, they were walking, not along the road, but in the woods, into the woods, deeper and deeper, drawn toward the glimmer. Over logs and around puddles, through the leaves.

Crutch—crutch—crutch.

Walking, closer and closer to the soft light, to the snacks and drink, passing trees that were healthy and alive, trees that were dead, trees that were different—strange and twisted, black sludge slithering around their trunks.

There was something on Billy's head, itching. He wished to scratch it, to wipe it off, but it didn't matter. It was there and he was here and there were snacks inside the house of Star Crunches and Sprite, yum yum doodle dum, and what did a little itch matter when there were snacks.

Billy and David came to the light—a clearing. In the center, amidst the glow, a white, rotting house sat, covered in thick vines, overgrown with weeds. Black moss speckled the porch, the rotting boards. There was an open doorway leading into the house, into the darkness, as blank as emptiness. There was Sprite in there and Star Crunches, yum yum, and songs, lullabies...*I wish I was in Dixie.*

Crunch, Crutch, Crunch, Crutch.

On the side of the porch was a lattice, unbroken, unrotted, host to a green vine and a flower. A flower as white as snow, petals formed like an infant rose...*look away, look away...*

On the front side of the house were two broken windows, behind which were snacks. Crunch, crunch, crutch, crutch. And the lonely old man—just wanting some company. He was tired...*in Dixie land I'll take my stand...*

An old man, lonely and harmless. Up the steps and onto the porch they walked...*to live or die in Dixie...*Across the moss-infested porch to the door...*away, away...*

Billy and David stepped up to the opening and were drawn into the darkness.

✳   ✳   ✳   ✳

The vision exited Perseus in a furious whirlwind. He lay on the floor, head spiraling with fading images—the intricate golden lettering, the lush grass, the silvery pool—vaguely aware of heat stripping his arm raw. There was slight pressure on his arm, after which the heat was replaced by coolness. After that came numbness.

The transient images of the vision disappeared and the real world came into focus. The numbness became stronger, tingling, burning as if his arm was encased in ice, and Perseus could smell charred flesh, a sickening stench that he loathed over all others.

He opened his eyes to find an old cloth wrapped around his arm, an oily salve seeping through. He was opposite the room from the fire, lying below the broken window of a rotting wall. The floorboards were cool and felt good against his naked body. Sarah was sitting at the table, needle and cloth in hand.

The wooden slats of the wall bent heavily against Perseus's weight as he struggled to sit upright. The effort made him sweat. The numbness in his arm found his stomach and twisted. Nausea swept through his body. Perseus tilted his head to one side and wretched heavily but dryly until the fit passed and his stomach stopped convulsing.

"You shouldn't have let me fall into the fire," Perseus said, laying his head against the wall, closing his eyes.

"Lucky you are," Sarah said indifferently, keeping her eyes on her needlework. "Lucky Malachai got you before your hair caught alight. I was out."

"You force me to hallucinate and then leave," Perseus said weakly. His stomach had settled and felt normal, empty. Cool night air wrapped around his sweat-beaded forehead, causing him to shiver. Perseus opened his eyes again.

"Not a hallucination; you were seeing events surrounding the Book of Antioch. If I'm not mistaken, you saw what you needed to. How the book was found...and more. Where the book is now."

"You shouldn't have left."

"Stop pouting, young one," Sarah said, weaving the needle in and out of her cloth. "You were in the vision for three days. There was too much for us to do to watch you." Sarah finished the seam she had been working on and put the cloth aside. She walked over to the cauldron that hung above the fireplace, dipped a bowl of stew, and handed it to Perseus.

Perseus took the bowl and ate. "Too much to do," he said through a large chunk of meat. "What do you mean?"

"We were preparing things…" Sarah said. "…for your journey." She took the empty bowl from Perseus, and handed him a cup filled with water. "You can have more, but we must finish our talk. Much to discuss before you leave on the morrow."

"I am hardly fit to leave on the morrow," Perseus said, raising his bandaged arm.

"The morrow it will be regardless," Sarah said as she filled the bowl. "Your arm will be healed soon enough."

Sarah helped Perseus to his feet and walked him out the door. Malachai was seated on the steps, a knife in one hand. In the other was the carving, which had nearly taken shape. It was a naked man, long and slender, with arms out to either side, making him look like a cross.

"One moment, woman," Malachai said, delicately touching the knife to the man's lower back, carving out the tiniest sliver of wood. He turned the figurine over and shaved a sliver from his inner thigh. This time, as soon as the knife left the carving, the dark wood turned to white ivory, the rough surface smoothed, the man's features melting from carved roughness into polished grace. "Done."

The old man smiled warmly and put his knife away. He brushed the wood shavings from his clothes and pointed Perseus toward the other side of the rickety steps. Perseus took the bowl from Sarah and had a seat. The porch let out a loud groan.

"I trust your arm is on its way to full recovery?" the old man asked.

"I don't."

"The fates willed a feisty one," Malachai cackled at Sarah, "didn't they? No matte—"

"I will give Nemesis proper burial rights tonight if I am to leave on the morrow," Perseus interrupted through a mouthful of stew. "I'll need an ax and directions to the nearest Laurel grove."

"That isn't possible," Malachai said.

"And Nemesis. Where is the body?" Perseus asked, only now comprehending what Malachai had said. "Why not?"

Malachai said nothing. He only nodded at the bowl in Perseus's hand.

"His breath for yours," Sarah repeated.

Perseus stared at the two in a moment of bewilderment, as a fawn stares hopelessly at the approaching shaft of a hunter's arrow. Then came comprehension. He emptied his stomach onto the ground beyond the steps. The few chunks that came were not enough, and Perseus forced a finger down his throat, gagging until he vomited again.

"That is enough," Malachai commanded firmly but kindly.

Perseus forced his finger deeper.

"I said enough," Malachai said and grabbed Perseus with his powerful hands, removing the finger roughly. Malachai stared into Perseus's eyes, forced Perseus to stare back. In the oracle's eyes Perseus saw a swirling bank of fury, which eased to compassion, though they kept their command.

"Enough foolishness, boy. The world is on the brink of unraveling and you are worried about your horse. Through his death you have been kept alive and been given his strength—strength you will need to complete your task. The fates have chosen you as the next warder of the book. We have only done as we have had to, as you must do what you have to, whether you like it or not. There will be more sacrifices, greater sacrifices you will make, that you have already made, though you don't know of them yet."

Malachai loosened his grip, allowing Perseus to slump against the porch's dying support. Weeds that had not been there before clung to the post, crept upward, unnaturally fast, unnaturally in the dark, breathing past Perseus, causing him to shy away meekly.

"It's as simple as that," Malachai said in a softer voice.

Perseus remained silent. He had no strength to argue though he wished to. And somewhere inside, he knew the oracle was right. What had been done could not be undone, and it may very well have been the strength of Nemesis that had kept him alive when he was so close to death.

Knowing this, he still felt dirty, impious, and wanted something to rest his ire on. If it had been anyone but oracles who caused him this grief, he would have killed them. But he could no more kill the oracles than he could wrestle the wind. Besides, they had only done as they saw fit; and the Furies had allowed it. It was meant to happen for the simple reason that it had happened. So then why did he feel soiled?

Perseus wrestled with his thoughts and leaned against the post, ignoring the growing weeds. After a time, Malachai spoke again.

"There is more to the story than we have told," he said. "Maybe afterwards you will understand the importance of your life as we understand it. This is no simple task to which you have been assigned.

"Nearly four thousand years ago, the priests who guarded the book were the only mortals who knew of the oracle's existence. When the book was stolen, thirteen oracles, including Sarah and I, were sent to retrieve it. It took us less than a week to track down the book. Yet mere days before we found it the thief did something unexpected; he wrote oracles into the book's history, lighting fire and brimstone amongst beauty you can not comprehend, putting our essence into a world in which it did not belong.

"The ancient oracles are no longer what they once were. Some lost their power, their essence filtering into your race, creating soothsayers and prophets—people with a fledgling of our true power, people who your race sought at the temples of Delphi and Dodona. Others were allowed to keep their power, yet were now guided by greed and envy. Still, others died.

"When the book was found, only three of the thirteen sent were left. The third gave his life to return the book to its original. The world once again found harmony, with one difference from before. Our race remained engraved on its pages."

Malachai paused, as if to let his words linger in Perseus's mind.

"Tell him of the priest," Sarah said in the silence.

"He is a fool that is dead," Malachai said to Sarah. "There is nothing more to tell."

"Then I shall tell the boy about nothing," Sarah replied calmly, and turned to Perseus. "There were nine priests who guarded the temple of the Moirai. Eight were decapitated, the ninth is no longer known to this world. I believe him to be the thief, but far worse. Far more dangerous.

"The book was found alone, atop a heaving mountain, open for the world to view. The ancient symbols were changing and spinning, almost to where we couldn't read them. But we could. And missing from the pages, was knowledge of the priest, his name included. It has been forgotten by the world, including Malachai and I. And we are the only beings left who have knowledge of the last age. In any case, the priest may have found a way to exist beyond the pages of the book, as the oracles once did. He may influence the world without our knowledge, secretly bending the will of the shadows to his. We do not know."

"That is a fool's belief," Malachai said.

"Then I am a fool," Sarah said. "Yet you should be wary, Perseus," she continued. "Wary of all that you know, in addition to all you do not."

The old man ran a hand across his aged, careworn face, scratching the beginnings of a silvery beard. Floorboards creaked as he shifted his weight. He waited until Sarah's words died completely.

"Since the book was found," Malachai continued, "Sarah and I have been its wardeins. We were allowed a brief stay from our fate, allowed to remain true oracles as long as the book was ours to guard. We sunk it into a window between two worlds to keep it from those who seek it. Over the millennia, few have found their way to our cottage in search of the book. None have left this meadow.

"And then, young David found it, quite an accident I assure you, and drew it into his world. The book now belongs to both worlds, although it may be nothing more than a child's riddle in David's. A dangerous child's riddle. For, with the joining of two worlds, parts of this one have leeched into the other. The *drakamor* in pos—"

"They're real," Perseus whispered, more to himself than to Malachai.

"They are," Malachai answered anyway. "The *drakamor* in possession of the book is not the only dangerous thing that has crossed over, but he is the most dangerous. Sarah and I believe that because the book is in another world, this one has been spared destruction. It is shadows that loom across the land, not fire. But these shadows still hold threat. They spread chaos, causing unnatural occurrences, causing an unnatural war. If the world does not die, it will surely remain diseased, war torn, restless, unless…"

"You, young one, are this world's only hope," Sarah said.

"You are the rider," Malachai continued, "a protector of the book. Not a wardein, but a warder. Your time in this will be temporary, but most gravely important."

"What must I do?"

"Deliver the book from harm and those who would seek it," Sarah said. "Hide it. Fail, and the world will unravel."

"Sarah and I have been changing faster than we anticipated—"

"But how?" Perseus interrupted. Against his will he yawned, his head suddenly light and wispy. "You have said nothing of how. And where?"

"We know little of where your path lies after you retrieve the book," Sarah said. "Only that it lies along the path of the Great Hunter."

"But—."

"But nothing," Malachai interrupted, and Perseus yawned again. His mouth felt like lead. "Shortly, Sarah and I will know nothing of our current lot, and the current lot will know nothing of us. Should we not perish, and should you meet us again, we shall meet you for the first time. Know that we may be dangerous."

"Time is passing quickly," the old woman said, her voice hypnotically soft, "and you should rest well before daybreak. Tomorrow you climb Taenarus." Perseus's eyes closed, his head drooping, resting against his chest.

"Sleep now," the old man said. And Perseus did.

UNWANTEN MEMORIE[5]

Rosy-fingered dawn crept above the horizon, bathing the forest in an orange hue and touching Perseus's face with its warm delicate rays of antiquity. He lay comfortably atop a pile of musty straw in the corner of the cottage by the fireplace, whose stone was cracked, crumbled, and cold. Dusty chunks lay in heaps in front of the hearth. The walls and roof of the cottage were deteriorated badly where they weren't altogether missing. The boards were rotting as if they had been standing unguarded against the elements for hundreds of years. Small patches of deep green moss clung to the porous boards.

Fresh air permeated the stale and musty odor of the house. Sweet scents of flowers came on the morning breeze tainted with undertones of rot and death. Perseus sniffed, inhaled the musky sweet scent, and allowed it to fill his hazy mind. There were pictures and words, memories of the past few days, but they were floating behind a veil, distant, unavailable. They did not seem pressing so Perseus let them be.

He stood up, wary, yet refreshed. The woolen blanket fell to the sagging floorboards in tatters. The bandage around his arm was gone, though Perseus did not know why he thought there had been one; his arm was as it had always been. He walked carefully toward the door, tiptoeing over the fragile wooden planks, past broken shelves and bottles and their spilled contents, onto the porch, down the steps, and into the soft grass of the clearing. Thirty paces ahead was a forest.

The naked warmth of the sun hit Perseus's skin and soaked deeply into his riddled soul; the warmth was like drinking hot cider on a cold night, and Perseus relished the moment, watched the butterflies and grasshoppers at the edge of the trees.

The cottage looked much the same on the outside as it did on the inside. Weeds twined around the porch's posts and poked up through holes in the floor boards. The roof was mostly missing, but where it remained whole, it sagged horrendously, bending under the weight of the sky. It was clear that the cottage's time had passed, but Perseus marveled at its strange allure, never before comprehending the beauty of death.

Around the corner of the dying structure, Perseus saw that the forest kept a distinct boundary with the clearing, which opened into a heath-filled meadow. The meadow continued for a hundred yards or so before trees penned it in at the base of a large mountain. There, the land sharply turned upward, climbing steeply and steadily, trees giving way to rock, rock to a snowy white peak.

Halfway up the large mountain, just above the tree line, dazzling black lights danced like fire. Perseus's eyes passed over the lights; they were just another oddity in the landscape. As he walked beside the cottage, his attention was caught by a spring that rushed out from the earth on the far side of the meadow; the spring's water formed a pool in a miniature gully before continuing down the contours of the meadow as a stream. It passed an old shack with a stone foundation and a waterwheel, which slowly rotated, water dripping from its wide oars. Past the millhouse the stream entered the forest next to a pair of young saplings. On the far right side of the meadow was a fence that surrounded a decaying red barn. Next to the fence was a small orchard.

Behind the cottage was an arbor, thick with green leaves and clustered grapes. Affixed to the arbor with a short fibrous rope was a pig, skin as black as night. The creature grunted nervously as Perseus neared and sat beside her, in front of an assortment of traveling gear.

Atop a woolen bundle was an unadorned sword and scabbard, an ash bow, a small leather pouch with three bow strings, a quiver containing ten full arrows, two shafts with points but no fletching, and six shafts unadorned, a copper axe, a small knife, a leather pouch containing flint, a piece of striking metal, and charcoal, three leather pouches containing copper, silver, and gold, three corked goat skins—one empty, one filled with a dark wine, and one filled with heavy milk—and a small ivory carving.

Perseus picked up the ivory man, studied its texture and intricate detail, felt its mellifluous contours. As he did so, a flash of memory broke through the veil that held all else back. It was of a pair of old hands, rough hands, hands that had seen much labor in their day. In one hand was a rusting knife with a cheap wooden handle. In the other was a wooden replica of the carving that Perseus now held. The memory gave no more than that, and Perseus placed the figure and the rest of the gear on the ground before opening the woolen blanket, which was not a blanket at all, but a cloak.

Inside the cloak was nine loaves of bread, three wheels of cheese, and an assortment of dried leaves, berries, and twigs, most of which Perseus could not identify. These lay on top of dozens of small leaf packages, no bigger than the palm of Perseus's hand. The sight of food made his stomach growl. He picked up one of the leaf packages and sniffed, tart sweetness, then opened it. Inside was a mixture of dried berry and meat...

...*his last breath to spare yours,* a woman said through the veil.

...and salt. The faint smell of salt almost tempted Perseus's light grumbles of hunger. But he for some reason was not hungry for the meat; it felt wrong, though he did not understand why. The wrongness was in the voice of the fleeting memory. It was not the soft texture of the voice; that had been pleasant. The wrongness was something in the words themselves.

Perseus folded the meat inside its leaf and set it with the others. He sniffed the other foodstuffs and felt no unease fighting his hunger. But before he ate, he took the empty goatskin to the spring and filled it. He drank until his thirst dulled, refilled the skin, and returned to the food. He dined on the grapes, bread, and cheese, occasionally in jest offering a bite to his tethered friend. The black sow, however, after calming down, had contented herself with lying in the grass.

Contentment surrounded Perseus too as he ate. He wanted not to move. It was the first time he felt happy since he could remember, since lying in his mother's arms while drifting off to...

...*shouldn't have put him to sleep...*

...sleep. He had been a boy then, and it had been pleasant. Pleasant then as he was now; the contentment dulling the unwanted voice till it was forgotten, and Perseus could focus on the warmth of the sun.

He was not tired, yet he closed his eyes, listened to the calmed grunting of the pig, felt a warm breeze drift across his nakedness. The scent of laurel came on the breeze, entwined deeply with the memory of his first kiss. Perseus inhaled the fragrance, lost in a dream, a remembrance of the beautiful young nymph.

Her beautiful blond, curly hair flowing freely down her bare shoulders, a light robe of satin drifting across her creamy skin, clinging to her as the wind blew, a gentle lover. He had chased the young nymph laughing, swifter than the lightfoot wind, through the forest's secret depths, finally catching her in a shaded grove of laurels. She leaned back against a tree, lips glistening, smiling, and laughed, a goddess singing, laughter sweeter than honeysuckle, laughter as there was laughter now, outside the world of the laurel grove. Except this laughter was younger, tinier, deceitful. And there were soft, quick pats in the meadow. Feet or hooves, running away from the arbor.

Perseus raised his eyes toward the noise, annoyed at the disturbance. Through the tall grass he caught sight of a young satyr, legs thick with course brown hair, back naked, head shaggy. Perseus's bow was in his small hand. The satyr ran in small, awkward strides toward where the stream met the forest.

"Ye'll be sory if ye don't stoppen,"[6] Perseus yelled, bounding to his feet, ire slipping into the olde tongue. The satyr looked back, fear straining on his young face as he continued to gallop toward the forest.

In a flash, Perseus was on his feet, running toward the child, gaining ground with every step. Wind flew through his long black locks as the meadow sped beneath his feet. The chase brought forward childhood memories. Memories of playing games with the other young nobles. Memories of hunting, trapping, and fishing beyond the walls of Larissa. Memories of flirting with the dangerous men and beasts of the wild. It was a childhood in which Perseus had thrived.

He caught the satyr close to the forest and clamped a mighty hand on the boy's shoulder, yanking him backward and off balance. The boy looked up at Perseus with hopeless desperation and dropped the bow to the ground. Perseus's hand, firm yet restrained, connected with the youngster's face.

Brays of laughter erupted from the edge of the woods. Underneath the laughter, separate, Perseus heard more soft patters near the grape arbor. He turned quickly and saw two satyrs running away from the arbor, small lumps clasped in their hands. These satyrs were much swifter than the one beside him; these were as fast as gazelles, and Perseus knew they could not be caught.

"What's the meaning of this?" he demanded, bewildered by what was happening.

The boy stared downward, dejected, and did not answer. Small tears escaped his eyes, pooled on his cheeks, slipped off, and were soaked up by the ground.

"Come," Perseus said angrily, grabbing the child by the neck.

Another fit of giggles erupted from the forest edge. Perseus's anger relaxed, was replaced by discomforted confusion. He stared into the shadows near the stream, searching for movement, a flicker of some unnatural shade, looking for somewhere to direct his anger. He saw nothing, however, and turned his attention back to the boy in his grasp.

"We'll see what you have cost me," Perseus said, trying to sound angry, unable to. He knelt and picked up his bow before starting for the arbor. Again the snickers erupted from the forest's edge.

Perseus's fury grew with the laughter. He turned to the boy, intending to scold him. But the pained look on the boy's face was heart wrenching. It was the look of someone who just had his heart broken. The young satyr limped slowly next to Perseus, breathing in small, pitiful jerks. And as Perseus looked, he noticed that the left leg of the child was slightly smaller than the right, the hoof turned inward. The last string of anger Perseus held broke. This was no thief.

"Have a seat if you like," Perseus said, nodding to the shade under the arbor. As the satyr sat down, still sniffling, Perseus went over his belongings. He sorted and shifted through the mass, found something new—a pair of clothes underneath the leaf packages. He put them on. Yet there were four things missing: the leather pouch with the bowstrings, the quiver of arrows, the copper axe, and the goatskin filled with milk.

"I didn't know," the boy said numbly, breaking the silence.

"What?" Perseus asked gruffly, surprised by the statement. He finished buttoning the black shirt and turned to find the child cowering in the sun. Fear had replaced dejection, and was frozen on the boy's face as if branded there.

"Please don't hurt me," the boy said, lower lip quivering, stronger tears threatening in his golden brown eyes.

"I'll not hurt you," Perseus said gently. He took a long draught from the water skin and held it out to the boy. "You must be thirsty." The satyr made no move, so Perseus corked the skin and threw it to the far reaches of the shade, where it nestled in the grass. "Drink if you like," he said, and returned to his belongings. There was preparation to do for the long journey home, to Thessaly.

…traveling for three years, but over twenty…

"Twenty years?" Perseus asked aloud. For the third time since waking this morning, he caught a glimpse behind the haze of memory. He had been speaking with someone about his journey. *Twenty years,* they had said. But it had only been three.

"Boy," he yelled, causing the satyr to choke on a mouthful of water. "What year is it?"

"Year, sire?" the boy managed.

"Yes, year."

"I…I don't know."

"How long have you lived in these woods?"

"I don't know that either, sire."

"What do you mean?" Perseus demanded, and was immediately sorry for the harsh tone. The child shied away as if struck, absently touching his face where Perseus had hit him. "Come," Perseus beckoned softly, sorrowfully. "You'll find no more harm from me."

"I didn't know," the boy said quietly, but not moving. "I didn't know they were going to steal from you."

"I know," Perseus said. "And you have already been punished for stealing my bow." Perseus nodded formally. "I am Perseus."

"You're the rider," the satyr said.

...came from the east, the voice said at the same time.

"What?" Perseus asked, confused at how oddly right the young boy's words felt. They were words he recognized, words that jumped through the haze of memory, but without context or feeling.

"The trees have spoken of you."

"You speak with the trees?" Perseus asked.

"The trees speak to us, sire. Or at least they speak, and we listen. Satyrs are taught young to read and listen to the forest."

"And what does it say now?"

"It says nothing," the child said sadly. "The last forty-two years have been strange. Forty-two years ago, the trees began whispering non-stop, something they had never done, speaking about the one who would come—the rider from the east. Then, twenty-one years past they stopped and the lights came."

Perseus looked through the lush grapes, up the mountain toward the strange black lights that danced and flickered. These too pushed a stray voice through the veil—*a sign Billy. I know it.* But Perseus did not know who Billy was or what the words meant.

"Those lights?" Perseus asked.

"No," the boy said lightly, but fearful, bringing Perseus's attention back to him. "Those are the lights of Taenarus. They've been there since the dawn of time. It was the lights in the old cottage that came, glowing fiercely and softly, sometimes only a dim redness. Some satyr's thought that an ancient evil finally awoke in the cottage. Some fled in fear. Some fled, saying the world had moved on."

"And you stayed?" Perseus asked.

They boy flinched, fresh tears threatening in his eyes. He looked downward, and slowly kicked clumps of soil with his deformed hoof. "I was left," he said quietly. "By my parents." The words were almost inaudible.

"And what of the others?" Perseus asked, nodding to the forest edge.

"Those who stayed," the boy managed to say, his breath jerky, the words quiet.

"Come," Perseus said, patting the ground. Shyly, the boy moved toward Perseus, clubfoot dragging heavily beside him, a tear rolling down his barren chest and into his thick fur. The satyr sat awkwardly beside Perseus. "What is your name?"

"Cyprian."

"Cyprian," Perseus said, and tussled the boy's hair gently. "A good name. Strong. You should be proud of it." Cyprian cried harder at the words, and Perseus quieted his tongue. He remained silent, watching the heath ripple in the wind, listening to the spring's quiet rippling and the birds chirruping. After a long time the boy's breathing settled and Cyprian took a drink from the water skin.

"In time it will heal," Perseus said.

"Or not," Cyprian said, and sniffed.

"Or not," Perseus agreed. "That is up to you to decide. Your wound is still fresh and so everything looks bleak. But there is another side. The terrible events that life hands out are only a test of your courage, a test of how well you can live through the cruel reality of life. You will heal and be stronger, or be driven to despair. Once you can see beyond the bleakness, I'm sure you will find yourself stronger."

Cyprian took another drink of water. "Thank you," he said, and the two fell into silence.

Perseus returned his attention to his belongings. "Tell me something," he said after a while. "What did you think of the cottage lights?"

"I don't know."

"And what of the others? Why did they not flee?"

"They are too drunk to care. They muse at the lights, saying it is something changed in the ale that causes the hallucination, or that they are reflections of the sun and moon and nothing more. All the better for them, they say. Entertainment the like they've never had."

"I see."

"However, this morning, when the light faded there was no talk of entertainment or the sun and moon. All those sober enough came to the meadow to see for themselves. I followed behind. They laughed at me for coming, and threw sticks at me. But when they saw you, they told me if I were to steal a trinket, I could follow them in peace."

Cyprian's voice trailed off, the fresh hurt apparent. Perseus did not wish to dwell on the subject. "The cottage was lit for twenty years?" he asked. Cyprian nodded. "And you think I have been in the cottage for twenty years?"

...*over twenty,* an old woman's voice corrected. Cyprian nodded.

"I am not twenty years aged since I last recall," Perseus continued, but was unsure. He could not remember twenty years passing, but he could not remember anything clearly just now.

"That may be true," Cyprian said. "Only seven times has the sun risen since the lights first shone."

"Seven dawns?"

"Yes."

"Then why do you say twenty years?"

"In those seven dawns, the forest has aged twenty-one years."

"How can that be so?"

"The world has changed," Cyprian said.

...*time is not what it once was,* the old woman finished, the old woman named Sarah, and her husband, Malachai—the oracles of legend.

The haze broke. In a surge, the veil lifted from the past days' memories, filling Perseus with remembrance and dread. What of Thessaly? What happened during the battle? What of his father? Of his mother? His sister? Were they alive? What was this war? How long would it take to return home?

...*time is not what it once was,* the old woman mocked.

Years? Decades? The answer was too long. They might be dead by the time he reached home, if they weren't already. *Twenty years.* And what of the book?

"The book of Antioch," Perseus whispered, hardly comprehending the words that left his mouth. "The lights." He looked up the mountain to the black lights—the same he had seen in the vision. "I must go to the lights."

"But, those are the lights of Taenarus," Cyprian said, "the lights of the dead. It's forbidden to go there."

"By whom?" Perseus asked.

"Satyr law."

"I am not satyr," Perseus said dryly.

He continued sorting and repacking the supplies that had been lain for him, slipping the cheese and bread into the pack, hesitating at the leaves filled with salt and dried berries and meat—Nemesis.

...*greater sacrifices that you must make,* the old man's voice taunted, *that you have already made...*

"Though I don't know of them yet," Perseus finished in a whisper, wishing against hope that it wasn't so. But Malachai's words repeated again, engraving themselves in memory, taunting and mocking Perseus with their unjustness.

Nemesis was before him, not as friend and companion, but as food. Nemesis that was given to him on his sixteenth birthday. Nemesis that carried him into the wilds beyond Larissa. Nemesis that had delivered him from certain death. He could not defile such a pure creature.

"Damn the fates," he said defiantly, and put all the meat-filled packets to the side, barely hearing that Cyprian had said something. "What?"

"You will die if you go to the lights."

"Then I will die," Perseus said.

*   *   *   *

Cyprian stood guard over Perseus's belongings, watching him gather wood, only fallen branches, from the edge of the forest. These Perseus laid in rows, which he layered, alternating the direction of the wood in each layer. When he had a stack as high as Cyprian, Perseus retrieved the leaf packets, and placed them on top of the wood.

"Tell me," Perseus said to Cyprian as he mixed a few drops of wine with an entire skin of water. "What do you know of this meadow and the cottage?"

"It is said they are haunted...*were* haunted," Cyprian corrected. "Few satyrs and other folk entered the meadow. For none ever returned. Yet almost all, at one point or another ventured to its edge to see its marvels. The fruit trees, grapes, and flowers were always pruned and healthy, the house, although rotten, never swayed with the wind or fell as it should have ages ago. There are dozens more things that are unnatural about this place. Unnatural, at least, without anyone to tend to them. Yet there has never been a soul on these lands as far as sight is concerned."

...the current lot will know nothing of us, the old man reminded Perseus.

The words struck a deep chord, and Perseus suddenly felt very much alone. Those he loved were years away, if not dead. And Andromeda.

"Andromeda," Perseus mouthed in horror. The strength drained from his limbs as the name washed away on the wind. Body numb, Perseus was a husk to the world, lost in despair. His wife was dead; for how long Perseus did not know. It was one of the most recent occurrences, and yet it was one of the last memories to return. Or so Perseus thought. What else was missing he could not tell. It didn't seem to matter. Andromeda was gone.

"If you will excuse me," Perseus said to Cyprian.

He walked to the pyre, poured the diluted wine mixture around it, and set it alight. But as the fire grew and consumed his beloved horse, the grief of his wife's death lessened, swallowed by the veil that held all the other memories. And so too was the remembrance that she was dead, or that she even existed. His past was already disappearing.

TAENARUS[7]

The sun was not yet full in the sky when Perseus turned away from the ashes ready to leave. Cyprian opened his mouth to speak, then closed it and looked down. "Why?" he asked hesitantly, and looked up. "Why would you risk death?"

Perseus checked the straps on the pack to make sure they were tight as he thought over the question. Was it for the chance of riches and glory? Honour and justice? Yes. It was for all those reasons. Yet none of these was the overlying reason.

"It is the lot that was chosen for me," Perseus answered simply.

He said no more as he buckled a leather belt around his waist and slipped the sword through the scabbard on his left-hand side. When done, he took a moment to survey the field—the small clusters of blue and yellow flowers, the long grass blowing in the slight breeze. In his heart, there was an overwhelming feeling of dread that he would never experience these pleasures again, simply, without burden.

And now that he thought about it, he was unsure of the answer he gave Cyprian. Everything had changed so fast after he first awoke in the cottage. Twenty years, not three, had passed. And in those twenty years he had not aged and the outside world had; A great battle had been waged between Thessaly and…And who? Or what? Either way it was only one battle in a war. Perhaps the aftermath of the skirmishes he traveled through in the southern lands. The world indeed had changed. Of his family he knew nothing. Of his wife and horse he knew nothing and everything; one was unremembered, the other dead.

His world had been shattered. Everything that had ever happened to him had been torn away against his will. There was nothing left from the life he knew—nothing he could be sure of at least. The only thing left was what lay ahead. And right now, that was the book.

Tearing his eyes from the field, Perseus turned to Cyprian. "You've lived in these woods your entire life, yes?" he asked, slinging the pack over his head and picking up the bow.

Cyprian nodded slowly.

"Then you shall be my guide up the mountain."

Perseus untied the pig's rein from the arbor and walked to the spring, using the bow as a walking staff. He filled the almost empty water skin, knowing the young satyr had not followed. With a sigh, Perseus corked the skin and began walking up the mountain toward the lights, listening for any sign that Cyprian was following. At the edge of the forest, Perseus finally turned around. Cyprian stood under the arbor, staring up the mountain, half in fear, half in awe. There was angst in the boy's face, fearing the lights, yet desperate to go.

"Will you not come?" Perseus yelled.

"It is forbidden."

"Yet you wish to go."

"Yes," Cyprian said, and hung his head. "But I dare not seek the lights of the dead."

"Then lead me as far as you might."

Cyprian's face livened, eyes shining as bright as the jewel star. "Yes, sire," he said, and ran toward Perseus with an unrestrained grace. "I'll lead you as far as the Alluvian crags. But we shan't enter the forest here, sire. That way is near impossible. We trek to the other side."

"So be it. But we must make all haste."

*   *   *   *

They followed the forest's edge east, passing above the spring. For a brief second, as Perseus passed the pool, he saw young David's face in the water. The boy's eyes were dark and frightened, and he let out a silent scream before the image disappeared. Perseus shook himself of the sight, did not wish to dwell on David's fright. He looked forward to see Cyprian entering the forest and quickened his pace to catch up.

The way was overgrown, thick with underbrush, rock, and root. The satyr moved quickly, weaving around obstacles that snagged Perseus and the sow, ducking under felled trees that Perseus had to crawl beneath, skimming over rocks that continually caught Perseus's boots. They moved this way for close to an hour, Perseus struggling to keep up, until a thin line of rock, which ascended the mountain, broke the dense forest.

"You move fast," Perseus said through labored breaths, and leaned against a tree. "We shall soon hit the Okeanos if we continue at this pace. I fear I am weakened from my long rest and need a softer pace."

"As you wish, sire," Cyprian said.

"And you will help me with these burdens." Perseus handed Cyprian the two goatskins. "Do not drink of the wine. Not while it is strong, and especially not while we are on the move."

Cyprian slung the leather straps of the skins over his head; the straps criss-crossed his chest; the skins drooped to his knees. Cyprian took two awkward steps with his new burdens. The skins banged into his knees, causing him to nearly trip. After a moment's thought, he tied knots into the straps, cutting their length in half. When he replaced them around his neck they fit perfectly.

"Very good," Perseus said to a smiling Cyprian, and handed him the sow's rein. Cyprian's smile faltered. "Now let's keep moving. I wish to be at the lights by dark."

Up and up they traveled, using the rockslide as a guide. Where it ended an earthen pathway began. This led straight through the trees. Oak and maple gave over to spruce and pitch pine. Steadily, the path got steeper and began winding between thickets of trees whose branches wove together close above Perseus's head, blotting out the light of day, which continuously slipped from the sky.

Though his burden was lightened, Perseus barely kept pace with Cyprian and the sow as they bounded up the steep slopes, occasionally cutting through a thick patch of forest to a different trail.

It was Perseus's legs that held him back. They weren't weak, but they were far from strong. It had been a long time since they had been tested. But nothing could be done about their fatigue, so Perseus put it as far from his mind as he could and increasingly leaned on the bow for support. When he could walk no farther without a break, he called to Cyprian.

"I must stop," Perseus said, breathing in harsh gasps. His clothes were soaked with sweat. The satyr, who was far ahead, did not hear and kept walking. "Cyprian!" Perseus yelled. The satyr turned, stopped, and finally walked back. He was cool and dry, his breath unchanged. "I must rest a moment."

Perseus sat on a clump of moss and took the water skin from Cyprian. He was painfully aware of the dryness in his mouth and the slight headache that accompanied it. Before he had slipped into unconsciousness on the back of Nemesis, he had been able to go days without a drop of water with his mouth remaining moist. Before, he would not have needed a drink, much less a rest at this point on a mountain. Now, Perseus gulped greedily at the precious liquid, and slumped on the ground.

Rocks dug into his back, but bothered him no more than if they were leaves. Laying felt good, and Perseus was tempted to take a nap, a short nap, something to give him a shard of energy. However, Perseus feared to waste the time, and forced his heavy eyes to remain open. When he judged that he could afford no more of a rest without reaching the lights by dark, he stood and announced it was time to go.

Cyprian led the way at a slow pace, allowing Perseus to follow close behind, attention fixated on the ground and each weary step. It was near dusk when they stopped. Perseus picked up his head and found the trees gone, behind him six or seven paces. A set of cliffs, deep purple in color, flecked with blues so dark they seemed black, lay before him and Cyprian. The cliffs were wider and taller than Perseus could see, yet straight in front of him was a break in the crags, as wide as Perseus was tall. Large rocks were wedged into the crack, creating a path that was slightly less than vertical.

"The Alluvian crags," Perseus panted. He retrieved a small slice of bread and cheese from the pack and ate it.

"Sire, it's not safe," Cyprian said, crinkling his nose.

"I must go," Perseus said heavily, and took the goatskins from Cyprian. "Time moves differently, and I cannot linger while I can go on."

He opened the water and drank, let the liquid replenish his strength as much as it might. Then he tried to untie the simple knots. Yet his hands were weak, and his fingers could not undo the knots. He tried to put the shortened straps around his neck and found their length uncomfortable. So, Perseus draped the leather straps over his left shoulder.

"I beg you, sire. Wait the night here, and begin at daybreak. Something foul is on the air."

Perseus ignored the words and hoisted the pig onto his shoulders. "Your guidance was masterful, young Cyprian. You have saved me a day at least. Shall we meet again, it should be as friends."

Without another word, Perseus began his ascent. He labored up the rocks, which were sheltered from the sun, making them cold. However, the path was easier than he had imagined. The rocks in the crack had fallen into place so that they resembled a set of mutated, misshapen stairs.

"Please, sire," Cyprian called from below. "It's not safe. The lights aren't safe. Perseus! Perseus!"

It was a strain on both body and mind to ignore Cyprian and climb. Perseus was tired. His shoulders were aching under the weight of the swine and his legs burned fiercely. He wished to stop, to call down to Cyprian, yet he knew he could not. If he waited for another dawn, too much time would be forfeited. So, Perseus shut out the pleas and focused on each shadowy foot and handhold, willing his body to do his mind's bidding. Each struggled, fought with the other, wearing each other down, begging the other to give in.

Slowly the ground grew distant and Cyprian's cries could no longer be heard. Perseus rested often the higher he climbed, but for short periods, using the time to stretch and massage his weak muscles. He would climb twenty feet, then rest. And in this fashion he trod upwards until finally, the top of the cliffs was visible.

In one last surge, Perseus climbed to the top and threw the pig onto the cliff's edge before dragging his own body onto the safety of flat ground. It was windy and bright on top of the cliff. The sun lingered upon the mountain's peak, and the breeze felt good as Perseus lay, head over the edge, heart beating thickly in his ears. Below, the ground looked farther than seemed possible. Perseus searched for any sign of Cyprian, but saw nothing. The satyr had gone back to whatever fate owned him.

Suddenly, through the deep thuds of his beating heart, Perseus heard music, a tune, beautiful and delicate. Without a thought, he was on his feet, moving away from the crag's edge, toward trees, their roots exposed but sheathed in dirt.

Through the vine-clad elms, the music, sad and lovely, made its way to Perseus's ears, drifting into harmony with his mood, making him forget everything but the sweet lyre and soft voice.

He trudged forward, the pig forgotten, the pains of climbing gone, passing trees of every kind: durmast and poplars, oaks with lofty leaves, soft limes, laurel, beech, ash, choice wood for spear shafts, brittle hazels and knotless firs, the ilex weighted down with acorns, many colored maples, the river-loving willow, water-lotus, thin tamarisks and double-hued myrtles, fruit bearing viburnums, twisted-foot ivy with tendrilled vines, pitch-pines, arbutus laden with blushing fruit, and pines, high-girdled, in a leafy crest.

Between the closely knit trees, animals and rocks were nestled, unafraid as Perseus passed, stepping closer still to the music, the leather straps of the skins falling from his shoulders, resting on the ground soundlessly, distantly, as did Perseus's bow, as he continued on till there came a clearing filled with spirits, ashen pale, male and female, weeping openly at the sad tune.

Unafraid, Perseus passed through the throngs of ghosts, to the far side of the clearing, where, seated on a rock, was the owner of the golden voice, a bard dressed in robes of fine silk, a healthy glow draped across his face. In his lap sat a golden lyre, as intricately carved as the tale he was singing. It seemed impossible, yet it was so. The bard's hands moved swiftly and skillfully over the strings, which sang along to his soft voice.

"I descended thurgh Taenarus life gate, in serch of Hades derken and grete," the bard sang in the old tongue, sweet and true. "Thurgh the thrallen wraiths and spirits I wente, mo grevous thane a dowves cry spente; nat to seken the derknesse of shadwe, but to speken with pale Persephonwe, and eek hir housbonde the lord of deeth, who comaundeth the unkinde reaumes heeth."[8]

The sun, which should have fallen below the mountain's peak, tarried, the last sliver of golden red remaining, refusing to leave the song to the night as the bard continued his tale, told of his wife's subtle grace and innocent beauty, of the fiend Aristaios who sought to violate her, how she fled. He masterfully told how, during the chase, his wife trod on a viper, her life forfeited, how he tried to muster the strength to endure the loss, yet couldn't. In the end, love had won and driven him into the underworld, in search of his Eurydice.

"Whan I cam upon the lorde and his queen, I preyen ther memorie of love keene. 'Yow too wert ijoyned in love,' I speke, 'if olden tales art not a wreke. By thes regne fillen with fere and grace, thes infinite stille realms, an honest place, restore, I aske, I halse, I begge of thee, the fate yelden to my Eurydice."[9]

Perseus was lost in the beautiful words—words that caressed his mind, coiling around it as a snake captures its prey, twisting and tightening until all else is forgotten. Tears spilled freely down Perseus's cheeks as the bard sang his plea to the lord of the shadows.

"'To yow art owed ourselven and the lond, for all persons dwellyng ther, I have fond, tarie a short while in conscience pitous, than quiken, lette or soone, to oon derk hous; heer oon way ledeth us alle in time; heer in the ende alle the worldly belles chimbe; over mankynde you kepe the lange holde; she too, whan rype yeers fyne growe cold, shall fallen and find youre paleys from above. The thyng I asketh is to han hir love, whilholm mo in my armen so bright, the wounde of los is above myn myghte. If the myghty fates wol nat pardon hire, I forsake lyf—mayst tweye deeths yeve yow chiere.'"[10]

As the song moved Perseus, so too did it move the bloodless spirits who dwelled in the underworld. Hades, even the Furies' cheeks were said to be wet with tears. And so, Eurydice was called forth from the recent ghosts, still limping from her wound. Orpheus took his bride, and climbed toward the bright world, on the pact that till he leave Avernus' vale, he shall not look back else the gift would fail.

"Nexte the sheene lightnesse I loste my digne strengthe, with murie so neer, at a narwe lengthe; my eyen wandren thurgh longen lust, dampnen my Eurydice bak to dusk; she fell anon to the hous of goosts, where tweye entre was refus by the hoosts."[11]

Tears reached the bard's sweet face as the final note of lyre died out on the wind. The last sliver of sun sank behind the mountain, causing the air to chill. And in the new light, with the passing of the song, the bard's countenance changed. Whereas before he looked radiantly young, face full of color, robes richly decorated, now he looked old and weary, hair blowing raucously in the wind, unkempt, uncombed, and filled with dirt, eyes pale and waxy, heavy, dark circles hanging beneath them, robes of plain wool tattered.

And with the passing of the song Perseus saw his surroundings in the new light, and was overcome with fear. Not only of the dead, but of the foxes and rabbits, snakes and mice, stags and wild dogs, which sat side by side as if their mortal plight had vanished from their senses, and of the trees, which were where none should live.

And with the passing of the song, the harmony, which brought these unnatural beings together, surrendered to chaos. Hollow, powerful groans bellowed as the trees began to sway and move over the course rocks, hastening from whence they came. Rocks of all sizes rolled down and up the mountain. The animals scurried and bounded in a panic, some cunningly slipping through the confusion, others not so fortunate crushed under root or rock, or between the two. The spirits awakened from their quiet seats and stood, walked westward in one massive army, crossing through the flow of trees.

Perseus was caught in the midst of the dead and moved with them, afraid of their touch. Yet they moved like the Furies themselves, unimpeded through animal, rock, and tree. Perseus dodged the chaos, dancing with death and life, weaving through the fray with heavy legs and weary mind.

A stag thick with muscle rammed full force into a tree, bounded off, turned a new course, and headed directly toward Perseus. Sharp, twisted antlers cut through the air, as the stag neighed and bobbed his head angrily, all the while building speed, running through the spirits of soldiers, ladies, merchants, sailors, and peasants.

Perseus looked for an outlet, a momentary opening through which he could escape the path of the fierce stag. In front of him a group of elms lumbered forward. Behind him came spirits, faces glazed with apathy. To his right, a boulder rolled to a stop and remained still, thankfully still. The stag came from his left, and bore down on Perseus with eyes of bewildered malice.

At the last second, before the stag's antler met Perseus's flesh, he jumped backward, into the throng of spirits. Coldness, not bitter but smooth, washed over him as the stag crashed into the boulder with a deafening crunch. Bone, blood, and brain splattered over the hard surface. The coldness effortlessly carried Perseus past the crumpled stag, continued to carry him as new thoughts entered into existence, into his mind, invading his will.

She could have no complaint save that she was loved, Perseus heard. The thoughts were not spoken, yet Perseus understood them, heard them, a woman's thoughts. She was weeping, pining over the tale of the bard, of the love that this Eurydice had received.

And then the thoughts turned spiteful toward the bard's love of his wife—a love their owner never received in life and would never receive in death. The thoughts spoke of the woman's end, at the hands of a long ago king. She had been tortured, raped, and strangled—entertainment for the king and his consort.

The thoughts struggled with Perseus, became life within his body. He was reliving this woman's death as she was reliving it, breath tightened, throat and neck afire. Perseus fought to keep the pain out as hard as it fought to move in. His legs felt as if they were being whipped and burned, and his groin became sore, sensitive.

Behind him passed a great viburnum. A low branch snagged his pack and tore it away, leaving the sword as his only possession. For an instant, as Perseus's attention shifted, the woman's pain receded. Then it returned, and Perseus couldn't breathe. However, instead of fighting the woman's pain, he focused his attention elsewhere, and regained his breath. The chaffing and burning diminished to all but nothing.

Perseus looked down and saw his own body walking limply through the thinning trees. Yet there was another body, thin and petite, bruised and bloody, that was his as well. Both walked in the same stride. However, while Perseus's legs banged against upraised rocks and his feet stepped into dangerous cracks, the bare legs walked as if there were no obstacles. It was a good thing Perseus felt no pain.

The woman that was him continued forward as if oblivious of this world and her captive. Had there been a swarm of panicked animals charging, she would have persisted forward without a thought to Perseus's life, and he surely would have been run through.

As it was, the woman's path skirted the chaos. And the trees were mostly downhill of the spirits, carrying with them the confusion. Yet there was one tree that Perseus glanced upon, a tree separated from the pack, which strode down the mountain, not in Perseus's path, but close to it, close enough that a stray branch bore down on him. He tried to move, strained to release himself from the woman. But it was only his mind that strained.

The young oak strode past him and the woman, knocking Perseus in the face with a stout limb. Stars welled up in his vision. His head slumped, felt heavy, almost went into blackness. But the blackness turned into pain, which thumped and screamed in terrible loud thuds, keeping Perseus awake, weakening his mind to the woman. Her last minutes of mortal life poured into him.

Screams pierced the air, the woman's screams. Her eyes opened defiantly to see the men gathered around her. There were torches on each of the pillars in the large hall, flickering and glowing—torches that had been used to burn her. Green plants sat around the room in large pots stained with scenes of mythology. She was on the cold, tile floor, naked, weary. Beside her was a large, rectangular tub surrounded by a short set of stairs on all sides.

The men's laughter was distorted, shifting, flowing, melding with the fire and ice that burned between the woman's legs as another man took his turn at her womanhood. This man bit her neck as he finished his deed, drew blood, sunk his teeth deeper, until a chunk of the woman's shoulder was in his mouth. He came away from her and spat the flesh in her face. Cold tears slipped down her cheeks.

Then the woman was bound by a servant, hands and feet to neck, and slipped into the basin filled with warm water. The bite marks and welts seared as if they were on fire. The king removed his robe and stepped into the tub, filled her with his wicked seed, and then pushed her weeping eyes below the water's surface so suddenly that she had not the time to take a last breath of air.

The scene left Perseus, was replaced by incoherent thoughts as the woman wept, as Perseus wept, until finally the woman released his mind and his wits came back. Before he could be exposed to the awful pain again, he shut out the woman's grief. He would have enough grief in this lifetime as it was.

Exhausted, Perseus looked up and saw the black lights were close, no more than fifty yards away, hovering above a depression in the mountain. Great billows of black, neither cloud nor smoke, burned brightly in the night air, lighting the darkening landscape with eerie shades of gray.

The dead, however, seemed to glow. Those in front of Perseus, nearest the lights, lost their pallor, their skin flushing as if blood once again flowed in their veins, their clothes gaining color so brilliant they could have been dyed that very day. Perseus looked down at his captor and saw her gray flesh coloring.

The first of the dead reached the depression and disappeared, fell downward, forward, toward what would have been a mortal death, toward what would be Perseus's death should he not escape. Summoning the last of his will, he focused and strained against the woman, fought to command his own flesh.

Twenty paces from the edge, half the distance since he had seen the lights, swift pain encased his left hand as it pulled free of its bond. He flexed and grasped the chilled air, reaching for the hilt of his sword. But his arm was not his, and he could only graze the simple hilt with tired fingers. Still, he strained for the sword, strained to regain control of his arms and legs.

Ten paces from the edge, and there was no change. Perseus fell into a panic, struggling blindly to separate from the spirit. The last of his strength hurriedly fled and, unable to fight anymore, Perseus fell calm. The Furies would do as they pleased, regardless of what he wanted.

He casually rolled the fingers of his free hand as if rolling a coin along the knuckles; it was the last freedom he would know in the mortal world. The edge drew nearer; the lights flickered and glowed; the woman's skin turn fully bright and colorful; the welts and the scars disappeared. Perseus opened his mind to the woman, felt her weeping soften, her mind calm as the lights blazed brighter, closer, no longer black, but white, serene.

Then, the woman changed, suddenly and forcefully. The lights diminished, almost to the point of extinction. The woman's calmness was replaced by tension. Her thoughts scattered, were replaced by a cold instinct, an animal instinct. On the air was tartness, sweetness, rot. And these scents were what brought the primal change. The woman sniffed the air, and the scent filled her head, Perseus's head, as if it were the only thing in either world that mattered.

The woman turned abruptly, forcefully, and Perseus was torn from her spirit as she ran away from the lights. He dropped to the ground, on the edge of the depression, and lay crumpled in agony. The sweet rot smell had gone, and Perseus could only smell the harsh sulfurous rocks. His lower legs were raw. His body felt as if it had been skinned. And with the wind whipping across his raw skin, Perseus screamed.

Sire, the wind called, and Perseus stopped screaming.

Two spirits, spirits that had been before him and the woman, passed through him, skinning his flesh twice over, leaving Perseus to let out another distressed moan on the edge of the depression, deep and wide as a chasm, looming beneath the black lights. It was as if a bowl had been pressed in the side of the mountain. A circular pool that seemed to suck the black light into it sat at the bottom of the depression.

Sire, the wind called again. Perseus turned to the wind, silently begged it to leave him alone, leave him to his death. *Sire, we must go now.*

Through bleary eyes, Perseus saw Cyprian standing twenty paces off, beckoning.

We must go now.

Perseus struggled up on hands and knees, flesh crawling with fire, the high wind fighting his every action. Movement after painful movement, he made his way toward the mirage of Cyprian.

Gradually, his flesh numbed to the pain, the pain of the dead, and began to tingle, as the rocks slowly passed beneath him and the spirits passed beside him. The spirits were amassed on his right, on hands and knees, huddled around a bleeding goat skin, one of Perseus's goat skins; their heads dipped to the ground, and greedily slurped the red liquid, the wine.

Toward the mirage Perseus continued, now aware of the mortal pain in his knees and legs as they bumped the rocky ground. His sword banged the rocks beside him. Three paces from the mirage of Cyprian, Perseus crawled over a rock sharp enough to draw blood from his already raw legs. The blood drew two of the spirits away from the goatskin.

Sire, Cyprian called as the ghosts closed the distance.

A strong, but small hand clasped Perseus arm, helped him to his feet. Wearily, Perseus threw an arm around Cyprian's shoulder and the two shuffled backward. Cyprian grabbed Perseus's sword and kept it between them and the ghosts as they made their way backward, away from the lights.

The spirits contented themselves with lapping up the already spilled blood. When the sweet liquid was gone, they did not chase Perseus; they turned and walked to the chasm, where they disappeared.

"…ts you," Perseus said wearily. "…came."

"I did, sire."

"Should not have…was forbidden."

"It was."

"Then…" Perseus swallowed thickly. "…why?"

"You would have died," Cyprian said.

The two limped away from the lights, fighting the wind every step, until a small rift, where the wind was not welcome, opened in the rocks. They gingerly climbed into the small fissure, as the wind howled in anger above, no doubt waiting for their exit.

Cyprian helped Perseus sit and lean against a rock before disappearing. Perseus moaned in agony for some time until he heard the satyr descending into the crevice once more. Cyprian set the torn remnants of Perseus's pack on the ground and sifted through the contents, came up with two packets of herbs and the cloak.

"Open your mouth, sire," Cyprian said, holding out three leaves. Perseus did as he was told, allowing Cyprian to place the leaves under his tongue. "Don't chew or swallow."

Bitterness filled Perseus's mouth as Cyprian rolled his tattered pants above the knees, exposing the bruised and raw flesh. But there was little pain as the cloth pulled away from the sticky mess. Perseus, in fact, felt only a sense of lightness, like he was floating in a dream world. He groggily watched as Cyprian tore off some leaves from the second packet of herbs, chewed them, and placed them on the open wounds. Then, the satyr disappeared again, and Perseus fell into a waking dream.

*   *   *   *

Sometime later, there was light, a fire burning at Perseus's feet, and roasting meat. It was a vile smell that made Perseus cringe. His stomach felt bloated and full, as if he had just feasted on a thousand meals.

A moment later, Cyprian stood next to him, goatskin in hand. "You must drink," he said, taking the leaves from Perseus's mouth and holding out the skin.

Perseus drank and then moved to get up, remembering the book. His head still felt light, but he was thinking clearly, somehow. How much time had passed since he had lain here? How much time was there until the world fell into complete chaos? These thoughts and none other entered his mind as he shifted forward, trying to sit up. His entire body felt heavier than lead though, and he lay back down.

"…must go," he said weakly. "Cyprian, help me up."

"You are not well enough to go, sire," Cyprian said in a voice of reason. Yet, underneath the reason, Perseus heard angst. It was as if the young satyr felt guilty for disobeying.

"I must go," Perseus said sternly. "Come, help me stand."

"No, sire," Cyprian said quietly, but defiantly. "It is not safe. You rest tonight, and then, in the morning…" Cyprian paused, gathering his courage. For fear of the path ahead or of Perseus's response, Perseus could not tell. "…*we* will go."

Perseus studied the boy's face, and then laid his head back on the rock. Cyprian looked determined, young, careworn. He looked too young and too old to begin a quest such as this. "…choose the path of death…willingly?" he asked.

"Yes."

"And yet you…do not know the mean…ing of the quest," Perseus said lightly. He did not wish to argue.

"I wish to go with you."

"There are…other paths."

"They are not for me," Cyprian said.

"…so be it," Perseus said weakly. "We leave at first light."

"Yes, sire." Cyprian said, face brightening. He pulled a flattened rabbit from where it had been roasting on the fire and handed it to Perseus; the fur was charred, the ears nearly burned off. "You must eat, now."

Perseus took the rabbit, knowing it must have been one of the ones squashed in the chaos that followed the bard's tale. Ignoring his churning stomach, he brushed aside the blackened skin and took a few small bites; his teeth crunched on the animal's shattered bones. Perseus set the rabbit aside and shifted uncomfortably against the rocks.

"First light, Cyprian," he said. "We cannot linger." Cyprian nodded, and Perseus closed his eyes. Within minutes he fell into a restless slumber.

∗   ∗   ∗   ∗

The sky was dark blue with the first rays of light creeping above the horizon when Perseus and Cyprian set off from their shelter. As soon as they crested the crevice they had slept in, the wind hit their backs and Perseus, still weak, tumbled to the ground.

"You are not well enough yet," Cyprian said.

"We must go today," Perseus replied. "Help me up." Cyprian made no move to help Perseus and stood in thought. At last, Perseus spoke again. "If you will not help me, then I will go alone." Perseus tried to stand on his own, but the wind swirled and knocked him back down. He began to crawl.

"You need me," Cyprian said and extended his hand. "And if we must go, then we must."

The black lights were visible not three hundred paces off, hovering over the deceptive depression. Against the brightening sky, the lights seemed even more terrible than they had in the night. Now, the lights were the only oppression in an otherwise hopeful setting.

Perseus limped forward at a slow pace, clinging to Cyprian as the painful stiffness of his injuries lazily numbed. Cyprian carried the pack, which he had managed to salvage, lashing broken rope with broken rope, fashioning straps that would only fit his back. On the straps of the pack were both goatskins, now filled with water that Cyprian had found while Perseus slept. The only possession Perseus carried, which he insisted on carrying, was the sword.

The wind pushed them forward, knocking them left and right with sudden, violent gusts. As they neared the chasm, rosy-fingered dawn broke the twilight, and quickly brought the sun over the eastern mountains. Yet the wind intensified, causing Perseus to fall over, taking Cyprian with him.

They remained on hands and knees, fearing the temperament of the unseen wind beside the chasm, and crawled to the edge, where they lowered themselves to their stomachs. The screaming wind picked up its fury, making it impossible to hear. Perseus searched the chasm walls for the easiest way down to the pool, and when he found it he yelled the plan into Cyprian's ear. However, the satyr could not hear.

"Once we're over the edge," Perseus yelled, hoping Cyprian would understand, "the wind will lessen, and we can talk."

With that, he slipped over the edge and stood on a thin ledge that was hidden from the glorious sun. His arms had recovered well, and Perseus hung on to the rock as Cyprian dropped onto the small ledge. Though the wind was less, it was still powerful, as if being sucked into the hole at the bottom. Perseus again yelled the route to Cyprian, pointing at it as he spoke, and Cyprian nodded his understanding.

Ever so carefully, the two descended the steep and long rock wall, expending the small amount of energy that Perseus had gained over night. Yet he pushed on with a will of iron, climbing down first, often helping the shorter Cyprian from ledge to ledge. As they climbed, they could tell that the sky was brightening, but the color was dulled, filtered by the Taenaran lights, making it tough to judge the time.

Eventually, the sun crested the rim of the chasm, and Perseus was thankful for one last look at it. However, as Perseus and Cyprian descended, the sun traveled as a sliver of light around the rim. When the sliver disappeared, Perseus and Cyprian were only halfway into the chasm.

Still they climbed downward, for hours it seemed. Yet curiously, the sky's hue never changed. And the wind never relented. And the lights remained the lone guardian over the travelers.

At long last, Perseus let himself onto the slim ledge beside the black pool, seamless and without reflection. Perseus helped Cyprian onto the ledge and they silently gazed into the obscure boundary.

"This is it," Perseus yelled, his hair rippling furiously in the wind.

"Sire," Cyprian said, his voice quavering. But Perseus had already stepped from the ledge, and was disappearing through the pool, into the world of the dead. "I'm scared," he finished anyway.

After taking a deep breath, Cyprian let go of the rocks, took a step forward, and was swallowed by the icy blackness.

BYNETHE THE WORLD[12]

Waking was like coming out of a drugged sleep, awareness taking hold slower than belief. Cyprian believed he was waking, yet it was just a thought on the perimeter of consciousness. He did not know who he was, or even that he had a body. He only knew he was.

Slowly, painfully, the physical reality dawned, and Cyprian felt vibrations. It occurred to him that they were coming from inside his bones, though he did not know why. The vibrations shifted and expanded outwards, and Cyprian felt his muscles convulsing, then felt his breath, finally a headache. His eyes opened.

He was curled up in a ball beside a cold wall of rock, shivering, but not from cold; it was warm here. Cyprian lifted his head, and the headache stretched throughout his body, then receded into the darkness. Along with it went the shivering. Cyprian flexed his small arms and legs until he was sure they were real. He turned over and saw rock above him and on his other side, an underground passageway. It was lit by an eerie glow that emanated from Cyprian. The corridor stretched to the right and the left, became obscure blackness in both directions, seemingly went on forever.

But where was the black pool? The walls and ceiling held no sign that would have marked the underside of the black surface. And just now, Cyprian desperately wanted to see the sun, or the black lights, even if they were filtered through the pool; he wanted to see anything but the cavern walls; he wanted to see Perseus.

"Perseus," he called into the gloom.

Perseus, the walls whispered back.

Dread chilled Cyprian's heart, causing him to gasp. Thick, stale air entered his throat, lingered, kept him from breathing for a timeless moment. Terrified, he looked about for the owner of the voices—a mouth, faces—listened for footsteps echoing down the corridor, prayed there were none. The rock, lit in a grayish blue tint that accentuated its sharp clefts and angles, was the only thing visible. Cyprian calmed, the lump of air releasing from his throat. It had been an echo and nothing more.

Though the passageway looked no more than a cave, it felt devastatingly worse, oppressive, stifling. And there was a feeling of power; strength oozed from beyond the strange light.

"Where am I?" Cyprian said to himself, and immediately regretted it.

I am where, the walls whispered, actually whispered. Cyprian scuttled away from the wall he was beside, and bumped into the hard, cold wall behind him, frightening himself even more. He quickly moved to the center of the corridor and curled back into a ball, closed his eyes, wished for this dream to end, wished for Perseus.

He had been able to jump through the pool because he thought Perseus would be waiting for him on the other side. Yet, between the moment he was swallowed into the velvety pool until he woke up, he remembered nothing. Not falling or landing or curling up on the cavern floor. It was the waking he first remembered, waking alone—wholly and singly alone.

"Perseus." he said desperately.

Perseus, the walls mocked, and then spoke from everywhere and nowhere at once. *Perseus is gone, now, gone to his death.*

"No," he cried weakly, covering his ears.

No, the walls mocked. Cyprian heard the words as if they were spoken directly into his ear and clamped his hands tighter. The voice spoke louder. *No death but yours and your own.*

"Please," Cyprian said with the little breath he had left. "Leave me alone."

Alone, the walls echoed, malevolent, mockingly, *and alone to your death.*

Cyprian screamed as a hand clamped around his wrist. He fought to free himself, but the hand remained steadfast. He flailed and kicked violently, hooves passing through the air, connecting with rock. His mind was wild with fright, fearing the creature that had found him.

Then, through his fear, Cyprian felt another hand on his head, touching him gently, almost tenderly.

"Shhhh," a voice whispered, loud enough to break through Cyprian's scream.

The walls echoed the voice, altering what had been deep and soothing into something menacing.

"Shhhh," the voice whispered again.

And although the walls continued to echo the voice, Cyprian felt comfort in the hand on his forehead. He opened his eyes slowly, peeking through small slits. In the murk, he saw the long black hair, dark eyes, and weary face of Perseus. Bandages covered the man's legs where Cyprian had placed them, and at his side was a plain sword in a plain scabbard. An eerie glow surrounded Perseus, lighting the cavern doubly what it had been when Cyprian was alone.

"The echoes are strange here," Perseus said.

Through the gloom, the walls whispered back in a petulant chorus. *Strangers are here, and alone to your death.*

"Talk only if you must," Perseus finished, and the chorus sang back.

Must talk if you must, now go to your death.

These last words spoke an omen to Cyprian, and echoed in his mind, drew a sheath of darkness over his thoughts. He was still comforted by Perseus, yet he felt no better about the gloom and darkness beyond. It was as if instead of being sentenced to die alone, he was sentenced to die with Perseus. Cyprian shuddered.

Perseus saw the boy's fright and gave him a smile, one as big as the oppression allowed. Cyprian smiled back weakly as Perseus helped him to his feet and nodded toward one end of impending darkness.

"Remain close and quiet," Perseus said, squeezing Cyprian's shoulder. "'Twill be a long journey."

A long journey, yes, the chorus sang, *but close to your death.*

*   *   *   *

They walked along the winding corridor silent, always heading toward and away from darkness. Twice they came upon an opening, small, yet spacious compared with the confined passageway. Inside these cavities were multiple paths leading in different directions. Both times, Perseus had stood and stretched his aching back while contemplating the roughly hewn entryways. Each path Perseus inspected carefully, walking a short way into the openings, smelling the air, tasting the texture, before eventually choosing a path. To Cyprian, it always seemed the chosen path carried them downward, further into the bowels of Taenarus.

As they descended, the air thickened and grew hot; it became difficult to breathe; their lungs burned. The roof sloped lower and lower until Perseus was no longer able to stand and was forced to crawl on his bandaged knees and shins.

Still the roof lowered and Perseus was forced onto his stomach, to pull himself forward. Cyprian was also forced to kneel, then to take the pack off and drag it along behind.

They soon came to a space where the walls closed so much that Perseus had both arms extended, narrowing his body as much as it would, and was wriggling forward mere inches at a time. The passageway turned, unnaturally bending Perseus's body as he struggled around the curve. Then the passageway straightened for a few feet, giving a moment of relief, before it bent sharply to the right, then back to the left and downward. It continued to curve without mercy.

"Maybe it's the wrong way," Cyprian said, at the bottom of a particularly difficult bend.

The wrong way is right, the echoes answered, *now come to your death.* This time, the echoes did not come from the walls; they came from beyond Perseus, beyond the light. Perseus said nothing, continued on, the scraping of his sword against the floor the only sound.

The tortuous passageway finally opened a little, but not much, allowing Perseus the freedom to move both arms and legs as he slithered forward. After what seemed like hours of moving this way, he came to an opening high enough to stand and stretch where the path traversed a black lake, thick and bubbling.

"The bridge of Acheron," Perseus whispered inaudibly.

The echo that came was nothing more than muffled and agonized moans; it was as if the words had invited the moans through a slim opening they otherwise would not have traveled. The moans came from the left, where the lake continued to the outreaches of the dim light and disappeared underneath the cavern's roof. Beyond this boundary Perseus thought was Tartaros, where dwelt the owners of the pain: cursed Tityos, Tantalus, Ixion, and others, if the underworld was yet unchanged.

Perseus put Tartaros from his mind and looked to the right, where the cavern opened outward, where the lake extended beyond sight. Between the lake and the far cavern wall was a narrow strip of rock—just wide enough for Perseus and Cyprian to walk on.

Perseus stood on the shore, resting his aching legs, wondering how much further it was to the ferry. A thin sheen spotted his bandages—fresh blood. The wound ached feverishly. But this was a far thought to Perseus; he was worried about the wraiths catching wind of his scent. He surveyed the lake, saw no sign of disturbance, though that meant nothing, and reassuringly looking at Cyprian before stepping onto the rock bridge.

As he crossed, he saw beneath the pool's surface hands that reflected his gray-blue light, hands that writhed and fought with each other as they clung to the water's small depth, hands that called and transfixed Perseus with a mesmerizing power. The hands reached up, but did not break the surface; they only called to Perseus with their will. He exhaled hot, forced breaths as he walked the bridge, staring into the water. How beautiful it must be below the surface. The smooth fingertips wove and bobbed, urging him forward, downward, into the lake. How peaceful. They could smell him. How soothing. They could smell his freshness, his lifeblood.

Perseus controlled his breathing and calmed his mind until he had reached the far shore.

Almost instantly, the fingers sped back across the lake, toward the middle of the bridge where Cyprian remained on the causeway.

Bubbles broke the lake's surface, the water plopping back down, creating horrifying echoes that died as suddenly as they sounded. And yet, as Cyprian watched, he saw no ripple from the broken bubbles. The lake remained still.

"You must move," Perseus said.

Move to us, the voices replied, *and alone to your death.*

"I can't," Cyprian said breathlessly. The words were hushed by the water and followed by silence. Then, from beyond the light's shallow reach came an answer.

You can't but come, and alone to your death, the voices called, louder. *Come to us, now, and alone to your death.*

The water broke in a deafening roar. A body, devoid of color, pierced the surface horizontally, lifelessly, and was carried on silken hands toward Cyprian. The dull skin glowed in Cyprian's light, fed off his essence. The figure hovered, came closer and closer, dull skin brightening. The corpse's eyes fluttered horrifically slow, and then its chest rose, slowly and methodically.

"Cyprian," Perseus yelled; yet the satyr only heard a clouded version of his name, and couldn't recognize the voice.

Come to us, Cyprian, and alone to your death the corpse urged, opening its eyes.

"Death," Cyprian said thoughtfully, numb to the meaning of the word. Yet it intrigued him all the more, and he uttered it again. "Death." Death was hidden behind the veil before him—the veil that urged him to come, to step forward into waiting arms.

Death for you now, and alone to your death.

Cyprian tried to step forward, but couldn't. He found himself moving away from the veil, away from death, and he fought the resistance. He was losing death and the beauty of the veil; they were slipping away.

As he was moved farther from the corpse, the urges grew less, faded into the water, grew angry. The anger pulsed, hungry and desirous for the interferer. And it wanted something, someone; it wanted Perseus. Cyprian felt an arm beneath his and realized that Perseus was carrying him, as he ran along the narrow shore.

The hands, once under the surface, pale but beautiful, were extended beyond the water, reaching for Cyprian with distended fingers, bloated and scarred, old wounds opened into swollen fissures, fingernails cracked and warped. Cyprian swooned at the sight and fell unconscious.

Bloodless arms swarmed in a fury, hurrying to catch Perseus as he ran. He slashed at the arms with the sword. Yet the sword could not pierce the lifeless flesh. The blade traveled through the arms as if they were made of air. The fingers nipped at Perseus's heels, going through the clothes, through his skin. What they caught was more precious than either.

Pressure, slight but painful, exploded in Perseus every time a finger or hand touched his ankle. The hands were tearing away small fragments of his essence, his light. Perseus replaced his sword into the scabbard and clung to a limp Cyprian with both arms. He dashed forward with a burst of speed and, momentarily out of the reach of the wraiths, searched the walls for an escape. The wraiths increased their speed; they were close, were nipping at Perseus's heels, hands extending farther from the water. At last, with fingers reaching nigh his calves, Perseus saw darkness on the wall at shoulder height. At first he mistook it for a shadow, but now saw it was a hole. He thrust Cyprian into the passageway, climbed onto a small ledge, and pushed the satyr forward. The lifeless arms planted on the shore, and slowly lifeless heads and shoulders emerged from the lake.

Foul is the stranger, they chanted, *and alone to his death.*

Three hands clamped down on Perseus's ankles, holding on, dragging him backward. He pushed Cyprian deeper into the small crevice and cried out as the hands clamped tighter, drew him off the small ledge. More fingers clamped onto his feet and pulled.

Perseus clung to the edge of the hole, and frantically kicked his feet. Three hands fell away, only to be replaced by four. He flailed again, and loosed a hand, which had been inching higher on his leg. But to fight like this would be in vain.

In one movement, he twisted his body and let go of the hole's edge. The rotted hands drew back as Perseus fell and landed on the blackened shore. The corpses fought themselves in a new state of blind frenzy. Those in front were pulled back, making way for other's advances, delaying the attack for a moment, in which Perseus ripped the blood-soaked bandages from his legs. Quickly, he threw them over the thronging wraiths, and spun, vaulted for the crevice.

The corpses immediately stopped fighting, and greedily watched the glistening cloth trace an arc through the gloom. A few quick corpses disappeared under the water and swam toward where the bandages would land. The others turned toward Perseus.

As his shoulders and chest passed through the hole's opening, painful pressure, a wraith's grip, groped his ankle. Perseus pulled himself forward, loosing the wraith's hand. His left knee hit the crevice's lip, sending a jolt of pain down his leg. But it was a good pain, a mortal pain. Perseus grunted as he pulled himself farther into the hole. But before his leg slipped into the darkness, beyond the wraiths' reach, a lifeless hand clipped the open wound on his shin.

An entirely new sensation erupted from the touch, and spread. Perseus was breathless, felt as if he was being unmade. Searing blindness came and went. Insanity came and lingered, then passed. The darkness meant nothing; the blindness nothing; the insanity nothing. There was no meaning in any of it, Perseus knew. Not in death, not even in life. Life was nothing more than a joke—a fleeting moment of consciousness before which was nothing and after which was suffering.

These thoughts alone comforted Perseus as he lay in darkness; his body grew fiery hot and swelled with unknown disease—a disease of the dead. It flowed freely in his veins, mingled with his blood, toyed with his mind.

After an immeasurable time, the fiery unknown in Perseus cooled and meaning returned, though he could not tell what meaning was. It was only a word that seemed important and tried to break through the throbbing taint of the dead—a taint that washed away all concept of anything but itself, until time granted Perseus meaning.

Through this gateway, he gradually became aware of more. His mind madly empty, unfulfilled, unwhole. His body stiff and sore where a rock dug into his back, stinging where the wraith had touched his open wound. The cramped passageway dank and foul. Cyprian unconscious. The wraiths whispering for him to come back to the lake, and alone to his death.

Perseus wished to cry, and did not know why. Tears threatened, and then left, and he remained where he was. Slowly, the wraiths quieted, though Perseus felt their presence beyond the opening. But the silence gave some clarity, and Perseus remembered the book and decided to move on. He cradled Cyprian against his chest, uncomforted by the familiar warmth, and crawled forward.

*   *   *   *

In time the cavern opened up, allowing Perseus to walk and carry Cyprian. And in time Cyprian awoke to the gloom and was able to limp through the cavern on his own strength. They stopped once to rest and eat, but neither ate much of the bread or cheese they had with them; the oppressive atmosphere seemed to keep even hunger away.

Through the tunnels they traveled, time passing on a whim, passing as if it were standing still. Yet Perseus knew it was ticking as surely as ever, whether faster or slower than the outside world he could not tell. Still, it passed.

And in time, Perseus and Cyprian came upon a light, lurid in the ever-present murk. The walls left them behind and the ceiling vaulted skyward. A hoarse whispering echoed in the thick air, accompanied by a low growl. Under these two noises was a gentle lapping, water caressing a rocky shore. A shadow passed in front of the light, followed by a dull thud. The whispering quieted. The growl, however, pressed on, circled behind Perseus and Cyprian, turned to a snarl. Perseus quietly clasped the sword's hilt.

"Perseus," Cyprian said nervously, grabbing hold of his leg.

Perseus, the gloom echoed. The whispering returned. The dull thud again sounded from near the light. Perseus stifled a yelp, biting his lip as pain welled from the wound Cyprian was holding, the wound that had been touched by a wraith.

"It's okay," he said through clenched teeth.

Okay it is, the chorus echoed distantly, *and alone to your death.*

Perseus gently removed Cyprian's arms, but kept one hand enclosed in his. It was the relief Perseus needed, and he let his lips loosen enough to take a breath of the stale air.

The closer they got to the light the brighter it seemed, causing them to shade their eyes. With every step the snarl closed in behind them. A sudden jolt in Cyprian's arm brought Perseus's attention away from the light and to the left, where the huge shadow of a cloaked man loomed over them.

"You've brought no honey cake," the figure said in a deep, raspy voice, pointing with a long hardwood staff to the darkness behind Perseus and Cyprian, where the snarling beast remained hidden. The figure took a small cake from a deep pocket in his cloak and threw it into the darkness. Immediately, the growling ceased. "But that is the least of your worries, I believe. The wraiths have smelled you for over a day."

The figure stepped aside, and let Perseus and Cyprian gaze upon the shore of a wide river. Bloodless corpses, hair wet and clinging down their hollow faces, writhed on the water' edge, half submerged, arms wanly extended.

Cyprian sunk behind Perseus and clung to his cloak as one corpse pulled free of the others and stood on wavering feet on the shore. The corpse was naked and gaunt, his skin sunken between bones, causing shadows to fill the empty flesh. Yet his flesh was seamless. His tongue came forth and danced over his dark, cracked lips. The figure lurched forward, moving over the hard rock toward Perseus, eyes fixed. The cloaked figure took one giant step toward the river, caught the corpse by its neck, and brought it near Cyprian and Perseus. The figure held the corpse just out of reach of the two travelers.

The corpse opened its mouth. Teeth, black and half missing, framed the sore-covered tongue. Puss and another dark fluid spilled from the sores. Rot and decay, hot on the dense air, wafted from the corpse to Perseus, making him gag; yet the smell strangely called to him. Emptiness filled Perseus and clung to his wound, which sprang to life. Fresh blood flowed down his shin and onto the ground. The wraith's eyes brightened with color, as it looked to the spilled blood.

"They crave what you offer," the raspy voice said, continuing to hold the corpse at bay. "The lifeblood you so freely gave their brethren. You are lucky to be alive."

The hooded figure picked up the corpse with one hand and took him back to the shore, where he threw him amongst the others. With a swift blow, the figure sent another hasty corpse back into the water before returning.

"There has been unrest since you spilled blood into the Acheron," the figure continued. "You are lucky to have entered a passage they cannot. Alas, it was a passage that led to my shores. You cannot imagine the pains I have had to put up with since the wraiths caught your scent again. They begged to seek you. They beg now. Because you have been tainted, they sense your lifeblood, and crave it stronger than the young one's. You have come willingly into the dark lord's realm. And for that I have stayed their wants till I know your purpose. I am Teiresias, prophet of the underworld, guardian of the Styx. Speak your purpose and speak it true, or the dead may know you yet."

The hood fell back from the figure's head, revealing hair that was well kempt and black, and framed a handsome face that was grimly set. And though Teiresias was blind, his black eyes were far from lackluster; they shined with mortal and immortal knowledge.

Cyprian and Perseus swallowed and stared at Teiresias. He had been a prophet in the mortal world until his life was forfeited and he moved on. In the underworld he gained great respect from the spirits, and remained revered by the living. Many mortals entered the unkind realm seeking his knowledge because every word spoken by his tongue was true. However, not all mortals returned.

As well as Perseus knew the stories, he knew this was most certainly Teiresias. Yet the ancient prophet was now guardian of the Styx, ferryman to the house of Hades. The world indeed had changed.

"I am Perseus son of Telemachus," he began reverently, openly. There was no choice but to do as Teiresias bid and speak the truth. To do otherwise would be foolish. "My comrade Cyprian." Perseus nodded to his side. "My travels have been long, and many have no bearing here. Thus, I shall start in the meadow at the base of Taenarus, with the oracles of legend. Many millennia they toiled in that meadow, pruning the nearby trees, herding wild flocks, gathering the meadow's grains and cotton, and guarding the Taenaran spring. For in that spring was hidden The Book of Antioch.

"I arrived at the meadow unconscious and near death, though when that was and how many days hence it has been I cannot say. Under the care of the oracles, life returned to my body as otherwise it would not have. Not a soul has entered that meadow and lived in over three thousand years. I was the first. For the world is changing as it never has. I was the first because I am the rider from the east. I am the rider spoken of in the ancient book. I am the rider prophesized to the oracles to come at the dawn of a new age. For the Book of Antioch has been found, and that dawn has already begun."

"I feared it was so," Teiresias said after a long, thoughtful pause. "The boundary between the underworld and the mortal world has loosened, causing great fissures to open, allowing spirits to roam the great plains of the earth once more. And mortals, mortals have wandered willingly and unwillingly into these caverns, as they should not, coming through passages that should not be. The book's finding explains the foulness to the world. These fissures. How Charon grew unnaturally weak, necessitating my placement as guardian of the Styx. It is no surprise at all. But what is your purpose in the underworld?"

"I am bound to the book and its fate," Perseus said. "Though not by choice, I am set to recover it and set things right."

"You?" Teiresias asked.

"I am the rider from the east."

"And yet you know nothing of what that means," Teiresias said, feeling the first odd and sudden burst of uncomfortable sluggishness that he had felt since before these two came into the underworld. "You accept your fate as if you know the outcome, as if you do not fear your path because you know what it has in store."

"It do not fear the path ahead because I have no path behind," Perseus said simply. "There is nothing left for me but the book."

Teiresias looked at Perseus quizzically, surprised by his answer—the only answer one could give and have a shard of hope of succeeding. He had been sure when he started speaking that Perseus wasn't the rider from the east. He had been sure Perseus believed the quest was his because the book said so, and for no other reason. He had never been wrong. And never before had Teiresias been surprised.

"So it is, Perseus, son of Telemachus, grandson of the grief-giver," he said, "and you, Cyprian."

Teiresias stood silently for a moment, moving once to shove a restless spirit back into the black water. He was tired as never before, and his thoughts were sluggish. This new feeling had begun when he took over for Charon, but had increased when Perseus and Cyprian entered the underworld. Increased ever more since these two came into his presence. And even more since he had just flung another wraith into the Styx. Along with sluggishness, reason, ever increasingly, seemed like madness. Madness, ever increasingly, seemed like reason. And even though he knew what Perseus was saying to be truth, it didn't feel right. Some force was skewing his thoughts, telling him not to let these two pass.

"Neither of you is written of in the book of the Dead," he said, eyes shining menacingly.

"The book of the dead?" Cyprian asked tentatively.

"Those who are bound to the earth are written of in the book. Yet you are not. For that alone you should not be here. You should not be mortal if you are not written of. And yet you are. You should not be searching for the ancient book. And yet you are. For that I should cast you into the Styx and let the wraiths drink of your blood." Teiresias paused, fighting the tiredness, the madness. His menacing glare softened, but he spoke with difficulty.

"Yet my heart tells me that you speak true. You are on a quest to set the worlds right, and it is a most important quest. Fail, and the chaos will grow till all is without hope." Teiresias's tiredness grew stronger, and the cavern swelled in thought. He fought to control his sight, and his arms went limp, unnaturally limp. Three wraiths exited the river. They walked unsteadily toward Perseus, and Teiresias fought his sluggish arms and mouth.

"I grant you safe passage across the river," he said, each word a struggle in itself. But once the words came from his mouth, a small amount of strength returned and the room steadied and Teiresias was able to send the wraiths back into the water. "And I will show you to the unknown pass you seek. Come quickly, for my strength grows thin while you are here. There is something beyond my sight that wishes for you to drink of the Styx."

The holy prophet quickly led them onto a short spur of rock to the right of the glowing lantern, which hung from the bow of an unadorned wooden boat that was wide enough for two abreast and long enough for Perseus to lay down. Wraith hands clasped the boat and rocked it gently.

Teiresias stepped in first and knocked the hands away with his staff, draining him ever more. Then he allowed Perseus and Cyprian to enter, and directed them to the boat's center, before plunging his staff into the water and pushing off. The boat glided roughly through the water, as if its anchor was dragging on the river's bottom. Teiresias cursed, muttering in the language of the dead, and pushed off harder. With a sudden burst of speed, the boat jerked forward and rocked, almost sending Teiresias into the river. The prophet regained his balance and hastily pushed the boat to the far shore. After landing, he guided Perseus and Cyprian away from the shore, to one of the many entrances along the cavern wall.

"It is a short journey from here to the passage you seek," Teiresias said. "But take caution. There are many side caverns that hold not what they seem. And at the end of the path there are two doors. One will take you where you wish. The other will lead you astray." He paused, sniffed deeply, and glanced at Perseus's open wound. "You have been tainted. Do not come back to the underworld as a mortal. The wraiths care nothing for your quest and will not let you leave whether you have fulfilled it or not."

"We are in your debt," Perseus said, "and cannot pay you for your services. For that reason, I hesitate to ask for a prophecy from the mightiest of seers."

"Then do not ask."

"I must."

"You would not like any I have for you," Teiresias answered.

"I would risk it, if you are willing."

"Very well," Teiresias said, and closed his deadly pale eyelids, which seemed fatigued as they had not before. When they came open again, the prophet's eyes were completely white. "Your life has been forfeit, though you live. Your death has been forfeit, though you are dead. Accept both of these fates or your quest is hopeless. Believe not everything told by foe or friend. Truth is often wrapped in lies." The words fell silent and Teiresias blinked; his eyes were restored to black. "Forgive the brevity of my prophecy; for there is great unknown in your future. And that which is known, is uncertain. But this I may tell you in full. Follow your despair, and not your heart or mind, if you wish to live and see your quest through. Farewell."

With that, Teiresias turned and strode quickly back to the shore. He stepped into his boat, plunged his staff into the water, and pushed off.

Perseus watched the bow's light fade almost right away. The gloom returned twofold—because of the prophecy, but also because of the sudden queerness that took Teiresias on the far shore and the fatigue in the ancient seer's eyes. Troubling was hardly the word.

"Let us be gone," Perseus said, wishing to be through the underworld as fast as possible.

*   *   *   *

The ceiling remained high enough for Perseus to walk without stooping, and the passageway was wide enough to walk side by side with Cyprian. They walked quickly but carefully through the gloom, wondering what surprises they would find at the side cavern that Teiresias had warned them about. They had little time to worry. The first side cavern appeared after little more than a minutes walk.

A rectangular opening, rounded at the top, was rustically carved into the cavern wall on their left. It spanned the entire height of the passageway and even curved outward with the passageway's ceiling. Black haze lingered at the entrance, threatening to spill into the passageway. A small amount of haze strayed away from the entrance, toward Cyprian, but vanished as it strayed.

As the two walked past, figures materialized in the black haze, forms shifting from one figure to the next. As Perseus watched, the figure of a boy holding a small bag of roasted peanuts appeared, and Perseus could almost smell the peanuts and the fire that had surely roasted them. The boy was at a fair—the May Fair held in Larissa, Perseus was sure of it. He almost thought it himself, but then the haze shifted, and the boy grew, hair lengthening, and flowing as the boy ran; the bag of peanuts changed to a bow, and behind the boy trees sped by, familiar trees, and then the haze was out of sight.

"I think that was me," Cyprian said, and swallowed. "In the Taenaran Forest."

"Then I think I witnessed myself as well," Perseus said.

The next few side caverns held hazy images of Cyprian's and Perseus's past, images that were vivid enough to see color and matched memories. Matched them and distorted them in a way that was disquietingly alluring. Each they passed, wanting to stay, wanting to return home, wanting their journey to end, knowing their path lay forward.

The last cavern stood out among the caverns; as Perseus neared, he heard voices, familiar voices; as Cyprian passed he heard a voice too, a woman's voice back dropped by the comforting croaking of bullfrogs. In the haze Perseus saw his parents and sister sitting by the fireplace, weeping for him to come home. And he wished to go home, wishing it far more than the other caverns had made him. The temptation was strong, but did not cloud Perseus's mind, and he walked past the haze. Cyprian had seen Niobe outside her hut staring at the stars, alone, and he wished to go to her. Wished to comfort the image of the woman who comforted him when no one else would. But an image was all it was. Niobe was gone. And Cyprian too continued forward.

The passageway kept level and straight, and soon Perseus and Cyprian came to the end, where two intricate doorways were carved into the rock. The doorway on the right was carved to look diseased, oak planks splintering at the tops, bottoms, and sides. The planks were held together by two rusted and cracked iron bands, which were also attached to hinges. On either side of the door was a faded marble column wrought with withered ivy. Between the column on the left and the doorway was a short stone pillar topped by an empty cauldron. Over the door, resting on the columns was a triangular roof, a flaking border filled with an image of the sun. Between the roof and the door was a slim space carved with ancient lettering:

$$\text{⸖ ⸖⸜ ⸝⸋⸖ ⸗⸜⸝⸍⸙⸚ ⅂⸜⸌ ⌁⸝⸍ ⸘}$$

The doorway on the left was hewn of the same design, but was full of life where the other had been dying. Wooded grains were masterfully carved into the stone planks; short round rivets were carved in the middle of thick iron bands. The ivy twining around the columns was healthy, almost looked green if that was possible; the marbled texture of the columns was brilliant.

However, three things were different. An intricate iron handle was carved on the left-hand side of the door, where none had been on the other. No pillar or cauldron was between the column and the door. And although there were symbols carved below the triangular roof, they were different. These read:

$$\text{⸖⸖⸜⸝⸋ ⸌⸜⸚ ⊐⸚⸍⸙ ⸘⸚⸍⸝ ⌁ ⸙ ⸚ ⸘}$$

"*Tessal*," Perseus whispered, and fell to his knees.

As the word died out, the doorway melted into real iron and oak, copying its stone counterpart. Richly grained wood replaced the stone boards, brilliant iron bands and hinges replaced their former, and white marble veined with a deep purple replaced the stone columns.

As the transformation completed, the door swung open. A field of golden brown wheat lay in front of a band of healthy trees. Behind the trees was a wide green hill, upon which lay a magnificent city surrounded by a high stone wall. In the middle of the city, at its highest point, was a grand palace. Back dropping the palace was one of the mountains of Perseus's homeland: Ossa, its snow-covered peak overshadowing the other peaks in the range.

"Sire," Cyprian said. "What is it? What does it say?"

"*Tessal*," Perseus whispered. "It is old tongue for Thessaly. My home."

Tears spilled down his cheeks at the sight, but doubled as he gazed upon his father's palace. Loneliness and emptiness filled his soul with longing. He ached to see the inner walls again, to feel the comforts of his large bed, and a warm bath. He wished to see his family again, the family he gave up for dead.

But if the palace was still standing, if this was real and not another trick, then the palace had survived the great battle talked about by the oracles. Thessaly had won. But how long ago had that been? Would his family still be alive? Was any of this real? If only he could there to check, to learn the fate of his homeland.

Perseus laughed sadly as he looked at the carving above the other door. The symbols were cracked and flaking, but he could read them clearly. He laughed again. This time it was a laugh of insanity. Teiresias, prophet of the underworld, guardian of the Styx queerness or not has spoken true.

Follow your despair, and not your heart or mind, if you wish to live…

Teiresias hadn't mentioned anything of home, of Thessaly, where both Perseus's heart and mind remained. This scene was real, and not some image in the haze, and at this moment, he didn't care if he lived or not. He wanted home, wanted comfort, wanted to be at peace. He was weary from the journey. Twenty years condensed into that of three. And who knew how many more years on top of that. How many years had he spent in the oracle's cottage? How many years had they been traveling through the underworld? He had come through desolate lands, desperate battles, scrapes, and scraps to reach the oracles, and there he had learned it was just the beginning. Since then he had braved the Acheron and the Styx, the whole of the underworld, and it was still just the beginning.

"Damn the oracles and damn the Fates," Perseus whispered. "And damn the world."

He wanted home, if just for a few minutes. He could step through the door, slip into the palace, kiss his family goodbye, a real goodbye, and be out before anyone knew the wiser.

Perseus sighed and sat forlornly, tears silently falling to the cold rock; he knew it was not possible to return home. Teiresias had never spoken untrue. To return home meant death and worse. With that knowledge came an utter hopelessness that Perseus would see his homeland again. His tears doubled.

"Sire?" Cyprian said.

"Quit calling me sire," Perseus laughed, wiping away a stream of tears.

"P...Perseus?" Cyprian tried.

"Yes."

"Why are you crying?"

Perseus sighed and rested his weary head between his hands. "We cannot go to Thessaly, Cyprian. That is why. The markings on the other door read *Taron*. Old tongue for Thaeron, where we are going. That is where we will find the book."

As Perseus's words hushed, the door on the right transformed into splintering wood and rusting iron; the cauldron burned into black metal; the pedestal turned to marble; metal hinges replaced stone. Yet the door remained closed.

Perseus gazed blankly at the door, his mind empty of anything but sorrow. One thought came from beyond his longing. He reached into the pack on Cyprian's back, found the purse that held the copper coins, and took out two. After replacing the purse, Perseus dropped the coins into the cauldron. They hit the bottom with a muffled clink, and then disappeared. The markings above the door filled with a golden hue as the oaken slab swung inward.

On the other side of the door was darkness, speckled with dots of light that looked like the stars themselves. Yet there was no horizon above which lay the stars, confusing the weak mind of Perseus.

Freshness not felt since entering the underworld slipped through the boundary, giving a hint of what lay beyond. Soft chirrups whistled through the doorway, behind which came a cool breeze, and the rustling of leaves. It was night.

Splotches of falling leaves blew across the stars, and Perseus finally understood. He was looking upward, as if lying on the ground, into a sky brisk and clean. Perseus stood with great effort, the exhaustion of the journey through the underworld finally catching up with him. Repressed hunger came on full force. He felt dizzy, sick, and wanted to lie down. Yet he grabbed Cyprian's hand and started forward.

As he and Cyprian stepped through the doorway, Perseus heard the other doorway—the doorway to his home—crumble and fall. He ignored the sound and took another step, bringing him completely through the doorway.

Immediately, the ground dropped away and a powerful wind blew around Perseus and Cyprian in swirls; the air grew thin and chilled, freezing the few wet spots that clung to Perseus's cheeks, then turned mild and sweet.

When the wind settled and the ground returned, Perseus felt lush grass beneath him, and Cyprian beside him; the young boy's breath was quiet and even, comforting.

Emptiness, loneliness, hunger faded to a dull ache. And the sweet smell from the grass flooded Perseus's nose, combined with the smell of the changing leaves—an overwhelming, intoxicating smell that lulled him into relaxation. He tried to open his eyes, but found it impossible. Instead, he found himself sinking into pleasant thoughts and pleasant dreams.

A Tour Sighte[13]

They slept off their long underworld journey in a grassy clearing atop a small wooded mountain. It was the sleep of a thousand nights rolled into four soft days, during which the weather remained favorable. At some point on the first night, Perseus's cloak found its way over the two travelers, protecting them from the cool air and the colorful leaves that fell from the changing trees. The next morning, sunlight bathed Perseus and Cyprian, adding pleasantness to their dreams, and all was well. And all remained well through the next three days, and even into the morning of the fifth when they awoke filled with warm life. It was this moment, this feeling, that helped Perseus understand how utterly oppressive the underworld had been. And how lonely, even with Cyprian as company. Here, though, the sun worked to erase those memories, giving hope for better days.

But along with hope came pain. Perseus was stiff and sore, his raw legs festering with blood and pus. It was worse where he had been touched by the wraith. There the wound seeped blood tinged with green sickness. Yet the fresh air lessened the wounds hurt. And the sunny leaves that flew across the sky helped Perseus forget his pain.

A large yellow and orange leaf with three oblong lobes landed on Perseus's lap. He picked it up and studied its silver speckled veins, turned the leaf away from the sun thinking it naught but a trick of the light. But the silvery hue remained. And from the leaf came a lovely scent, born of saffron. Perseus luxuriated in the sweet cadence of the aroma till it washed him of the last remnant of pain, refreshing him with hope.

And along with hope came ravenous hunger and thirst. He and Cyprian had been hungry for how long that they had not filled their bellies? Thirsty for how long that they had not wetted their tongues? Neither could tell, but they knew the hunger and thirst was right. It had been long.

And along with hope came a new start.

"I feel strange," Cyprian said, as Perseus dug through the pack.

"It is life," Perseus replied, "returned to you as it was stolen."

"Has it always been this coarse?" Cyprian asked, holding up an arm, inspecting it in the light. "I feel as if I've been shaken and put through a grindstone. Look at how my arm wavers."

The arm was indeed shaking slightly, minutely, but utterly fast. Perseus removed two wheels of cheese and a loaf of bread before looking at Cyprian's arm. He mused over the small hand, then looked at his own arm, which was also slightly shaking.

"It does feel strange," Perseus said, and returned to emptying the pack. "And rough. As if we've been reborn and must face the world for the first time." A wheel of cheese slipped from Perseus's hand and grazed his wound before hitting the ground. He grimaced and held his breath as his leg throbbed with a deep ache. "I suppose it is," he said through clenched teeth. "Coarse that is." Perseus took a short breath and grabbed his leg above the wound. "But I imagine we never noticed it before because we're used to it." He took a longer breath followed by a series of short breaths and released his leg. "Pain is how we know we're alive."

"Those need treatment," Cyprian said. "They're infected."

"So they are," Perseus said, the pain steady, his breath returning to normal. "But I don't have the skill."

"Do not worry about that," Cyprian said, and scooted over to the pack. He dug down and pulled out a small bunch of dried twigs, leaves, and berries that were tied together with twine. From the bunch he pulled off the leaves and berries, combined them with a dab of water, and ground them into a violet paste. This, he used to cover Perseus's wounds. Almost immediately, Perseus felt the cooling effect of the ointment. The pain grew dull, and then numb.

"Again you have proven yourself more than you seem," Perseus said. "I am deeply indebted. I shall hate to lose a companion such as you."

"Lose me?" Cyprian asked, confused.

"You have come far already, Cyprian. But there will come a time when you must decide your part in this quest. Let us not talk of such things just yet, though. It is a glorious morning, and there is much to catch up on that we missed while in the underworld.

Cyprian nodded, unable to argue as Perseus removed the last of the food from the pack. They gorged on sweet cheese and bread, slaking their thirst from the water skin between mouthfuls, all the while gazing about this new world, both strange and familiar.

The clearing was a bumpy bit of land covered with grass as plush as the finest bearskins. Rocks the size of Cyprian sprung from the ground in odd places, and two trees, long ago felled, lay at the edge of the wood. Perseus and Cyprian had slept in an almost level space in the center of the clearing next to a flat slab of granite that was depressed into the rich ground.

Perseus wiped the leaves clear of the stone, and found it carved with markings. A circle, almost central to the stone, was surrounded by two other circles and a multitude of lines, straight and meandering, narrow and wide. The markings were familiar to Perseus, but he did not remember how.

The surrounding woods, meanwhile, had mesmerized Cyprian. The hardwood trees were tall and strong, trunks thick, branches twining together. And a wonder he had never seen before—all the trees were in color at the same time, an event unthinkable in the Taenaran forest. There the trees changed color only once, when their time had passed. Still, Cyprian understood that these changing colors did not mean death. These trees would shed and then grow anew next year.

Sweet flowers—long hollow shafts of deep red and orange, flowing to fluted petal edges of fiery yellow—hung from the vines, and were backset by leaves of the darkest green. Large fruit also hung from many of the vines and looked more delicious than anything Cyprian had eaten, certainly more delicious than the current meal. The fruit was oblong, its skin green and interspersed with flecks of honey molten orange. Their sweetness wafted toward Cyprian on a slight breeze. He swallowed thickly, the last of his dry cheese and stale bread tasting and feeling like grit as it went down his throat. He pointed at the fruit, his hunger unabated, mouth salivating.

"What about those?" he asked Perseus, a strange glaze over his eyes. "They look edible."

Cyprian stood, eyes unmoved from the fruit. Perseus grabbed him by the arm and pulled him gently to a sit. "Those are not for us," he said, and pointed to four places in the thicket. He too had seen the fruit. But he had also looked through the vine-clad darkness into the recesses of shadow and seen the ancient stones. "Look beyond the vines, Cyprian, and you will see four unnatural stones. The fruit is sacred to this place."

Cyprian searched the forest where Perseus had pointed, but found it difficult to focus on anything beyond the vines. His eyes were drawn to the succulent, juicy fruit, surely the food of the gods. He yearned for the fruit, could taste the sweetness already. Even as these thoughts came, he focused harder, forced his eyes into the shadow they did not wish to go, and finally saw the forest interlopers.

The rocks were set equidistant from each other, as if on the corners of a square, and were surrounded by thin webs of translucent fiber, through which Cyprian could barely see the ancient symbols. "What do they say?" he asked.

"Each symbol represents one of the four winds. There is north," Perseus said, and pointed to his right. Cyprian strained to see the symbol; it shied away from his vision as if it did not want to be seen. Perseus then pointed to the other stones. "There is west, south, and east."

"But it is odd, Cyprian. This is an ancient shrine to the dead, in order with the customs of our world. So ancient I've only read about them in parchments."

Perseus stood thoughtfully and surveyed the granite slab. Its elegantly simplistic markings pulled at a thread of knowledge hidden in his mind, knowledge from his childhood lessons at the Tower of Byblis. He walked around the rock, slowly at first, mumbling: "Yes, yes, I see it. A map." Then he paced faster, as understanding dawned on him.

"There was a great battle," he said, beckoning Cyprian to join him. "We are here." Perseus pointed to the largest circle, which was the eastern most of the three. Around it were the symbols of the winds. "This is Thaeron, and these markings are the wind stones. Though the battle did not happen here. Over here is where the battle took place." Perseus pointed to the two other circles on the stone, and a slew of hash marks that ran in between. He gazed northward, but could not see the other hills through the trees and went back to the slab. "Great armies fought hand to hand, at these lines." Perseus pointed to the many-segmented lines between the two smaller circles. He stopped and listened to a quiet gust of wind that felt oddly energized. "These are hallowed grounds, Cyprian."

He paused and looked at the large circle and the surrounding marks. Then, almost in alarm, Perseus lifted his head and searched the woods near the ancient stones.

"Though this is a shrine of our world," he said, watching the keen darkness. "but the battle happened in this one. It is odd that our world has leeched into this one and given over its attributes. The oracles never…" Perseus continued the thought in his head, wondering why the oracles didn't mention that the two worlds were morphing together. He wondered if they even knew.

"We leave as soon as possible. I wish to be as far from these grounds as possible by the end of the day. This place is a hybrid of two worlds, and for that we should be wary. All the more because it has ties to the underworld. I do not wish to see what will come after dark. Come, gather your things. The fates have kept us safe thus far. Let's not push their favor."

"Yes, sire," Cyprian said, scared by the sudden change in Perseus's demeanor, and began to gather his pack.

"Cyprian."

"Yes, sire?"

"Do not call me sire," Perseus said warmly, and smiled. "Perseus. You will call me Perseus."

The smile momentary eased Cyprian's fright. "Yes, sire…Perseus," he said. "Perseus?"

"Yes."

"Where is it that we are going?"

"West, my friend. West."

And alone to your death, Cyprian finished in his mind.

"To the house of a *drakamor,*" Perseus said.

"A *drakamor?*"

"It does not translate well, but it literally means great spirit. Yet *draka,* in the old tongue was understood differently than in the modern. A *draka* was a spirit that is wholly evil, soulless, and malicious."

"Sounds…" Cyprian swallowed, as he picked up the pack. "Sounds fun." He laughed nervously.

"It will be anything but," Perseus said. "But we will talk about that later."

He put an arm around on the satyr's shoulder, and they walked away from the clearing, taking care not to disturb the vines beyond what was needed. In less than a minute, the landscape changed. Not in form or beauty, but in sheen. The trees, leaves, and ground once shimmering, now only shined. The colors were still clear, but somehow they were different; away from the top of the mountain, they were less brilliant, as were the smells, and the feel of the air. Cyprian noticed the change, but said nothing. Only when they came to a rock outcropping, where the lay of the land could be seen, where Cyprian could see the disquieting change as well, did he speak the obvious.

"It's different," he said.

At the base of the mountain the land rolled with woods, farmland, and field. Two cottages, separated by more than a mile, were visible. And though no road could be seen, there were thin, continuous breaks in the woods, which could only be for roads. The scene would have looked normal had it not been marbled with colors as sharp and bright as those on the mountain's top.

"So it is," Perseus agreed.

"What is it?"

"If I were to guess," Perseus said, "I would say it is the meeting of the two worlds."

"I don't like it."

"Neither do I. But it's what lies ahead"

Purple mountains marked the distant horizon. In front of the mountains, not more than two or three miles from Thaeron was a row of trees on a small ridge. An unnatural shape with sharp edges filled a disruption in the trees directly in front of Perseus; it was square and had a slanted roof. Perseus judged it a tower or other ruins of some kind, and pointed it out to Cyprian.

"We should make it there by nightfall," he said, "if we are fast."

"Then we'd better get moving," Cyprian replied without enthusiasm.

Nigh a quarter way down the mountain they came upon a spring-fed pool. As Perseus drank, he marveled at his horrid reflection. His eyes were sunken and dark, his skin gaunt and pale. Life within his body was but a hint of what it had been, and Perseus drank until his stomach was bloated and cramped. Yet Perseus was satisfied with the pain; he knew he was alive.

Although the draught made him sleepy, he and Cyprian left the pool. When they came to the first spot of brilliant land the air turned crisp and the trees shimmered. At the boundary's edge a raven sat in the air bound treetops. Its black coat glistened terribly, and its beak was the brightest orange Perseus had ever seen.

The raven keenly eyed the travelers, unafraid as they passed below, and even offered a loud squawk that caused Cyprian to stumble and fall. Cyprian grabbed a rock, stood, and threw, missing the bird by less than a foot. The bird remained unmoved.

"Stupid bird," he muttered.

"Smarter than you'd think," Perseus said. "He rattled you by doing no more than sitting still."

"It's not him," Cyprian replied. "It's this place."

"I know, I know," Perseus said. "It's unnerving. But only because it's unknown. You must learn to not let fear consume your thoughts when the phantoms you see are only in your mind. Of this land, be wary. Be wary of everything and anything. But do not fear it."

A branch fell deep in the woods. Cyprian spun toward the noise and stared into the stillness. "I...I don't know if I can."

"You can if you wish to," Perseus replied. "All you have to do is put your mind to it. Have you ever heard the tale of Daedalus?"

"No," Cyprian said.

"It's the tale of a man who did the impossible because he believed he could."

"Did he have to travel through a strange land with horrid creatures?"

"In some ways, yes," Perseus replied. "For the ancient world in which Daedalus lived was full of many horrors not known today. But that is not the point of the tale. Listen and you shall hear.

"Daedalus was a master architect...

*   *   *   *

...yet his skill reached far beyond. His craft was an unimagined art, building and fashioning structures and devices, designs of which the world had never seen. Yet Daedalus was mortal and not god. Driven by jealousy, he slayed his prodigy nephew and was banished from his beloved home. He took refuge under the rule of the great king Minos on the island fortress of Crete. Here, in the city of Knossos, Daedalus found both luck and misfortune.

He lodged in the palace of Minos, which was set atop a steep cliff that looked seaward. The king allowed Daedalus to practice his skill freely, and contracted him for many projects, the first of which was the restoration of Titos, a remnant giant of the Bronze Age. When this project was completed successfully, a project unfinished by countless artisans and engineers, Minos at last knew the true skill of Daedalus, and conceived a plan to keep him on the isle.

A woman was quickly found for the architect, and he soon grew to love her, as was Minos's design. They wed on the third anniversary of Daedalus's arrival on Crete and conceived a son that very night.

Nine months later the mother died during the birthing, and Daedalus was left with a son and sorrow. Pining to be away from his grief, the architect made plans to leave the isle to find new adventure. The night before his journey, however, he was invited to dine with the king. He arrived at the banquet hall promptly at six o'clock, and he and Minos ate and drank with the merriment associated with fond farewells.

"Daedalus," the king said, as the feast drew to a close, "you are a great man among men. Your skill is paralleled by none, and you have wrought this household wonders the world has never dreamed. Friendship has grown between us, and I am fond of your company. It would be a sad day that you left. Please, reconsider your decision. There are other women on Crete. All of them at your disposal if you would but choose. I will ask you this once to remain in my council."

"My king," Daedalus answered respectively, "much heartache do I associate with Crete, but not on your Majesty's account. I love you like a father. But my heart weeps while confined within these walls. Phaidra was my life here, and now she is my death. I do not wish to leave, but it must be so. New life can only be found elsewhere."

The king sat back in his chair and sighed. "'Tis your last word?" he asked.

"Yes."

"It grieves me so," Minos answered. At that moment, the doors to the hall opened. Three armed soldiers walked into the room and surrounded Daedalus's chair. "I would be a fool to myself to lose a friend over such petty matters as women and love. And I would be a fool to my kingdom to lose such a craftsman. I am sorry, my friend."

The guards whisked Daedalus to a choice set of apartments overlooking the garden of the Hesperides and the sea. Minos set forth Titos to guard the isle from Daedalus's escape. Three times the giant walked the island in a day, and Daedalus watched it from his lofty apartment with his infant son.

The years passed and Daedalus was consulted on projects for the king and the queen, and was often let out of his prison to oversee their construction. Thus was built protection for the courtyard of the Hesperides and the Labyrinth beneath the city, and the finest hanging gardens in all the world, for which both Pasiphae and Minos were grateful.

In time, the boy Icarus grew to be a young man, oblivious of his captivity—for he knew no better; the steep walls were a toy to his shining eyes; the hidden alcoves and underground passageways of the palace gave the boy more adventure than he had time for; the orchards offered trees to climb and fruit to eat; and the masterfully woven tapestries on the prison walls served as entertainment and education alike.

Hours on end, father would teach son the history of the land, using the tapestries as guide. One in particular, a tapestry woven so skillful it matched Daedalus's own craft, showed the gods deceived and deceiving, and was Daedalus's favorite. This he used to teach:

Europa cheated by Zeus in a bull's disguise; the girl sat upon the bull as Jove carried her through the sea, she drawing her feet up in fear, dreading the frothing billows' touch, gazing to the shore. And Asterie in the struggling eagle's clutch, and Leda lying under the white swan's wings, and also tricking Antiope, Alcmena, Danae, Aegina, and as a spotted serpent Proserpine. Poseidon next in his deceitful guises—a savage bull, a ram, a horse, and a dolphin. On to Phoebus in a herdsman's guise, as a lion, and as a hawk, how he fooled one of Diana's nymphs, with his elegant plumage that looked like real feathers, a real hawk you'd think; feathers lain upon feathers to form a growing graded shape, as rustic pipes rose in a gradual slope of lengthening reeds. Phoebus in this brilliant manner led the nymph away from her troop to do as he pleased. And Dionyses with a bunch of grapes fooling Erigone. All was wrought amongst a narrow band of flowers sprouted from ivy.

Daedalus kept his son by the tapestry for hours, recounting the tales of the past, for his own pleasure, and the boy's; for Icarus found much pleasure in them too, and wanted to hear the tales as often as his father would tell them.

When Daedalus was through recounting, up to the captive walls went the two to catch lonely feathers on the wandering breeze. And Daedalus would stare at the sea and the bronze guardian, and pine for freedom for himself and the boy.

In the first year of the boy's manhood, Daedalus set his mind on escape; the boy was beginning to show signs of malcontent, needing to be free from his unearned cage.

'Though land and sea,' Daedalus thought, 'The king may bar to me, at least the sky is mine; through it I'll set my course divine. Minos may own all else there, but he does not own the air.'

He worked his craft laboriously, laying row upon row of feathers, smallest ones first, followed by the larger ones. Then, binding the middle and the base with wax and flaxen threads, Daedalus bent the feathers into a gentle curve to imitate the wings of a bird.

The old man's cheeks were wet, the father's hands trembling as he prepared his son's wings. 'Fly between the heavens and the earth,' he said. 'Watch not Orion's sword with mirth, All this said to you, I plead. Set your course where I shall lead.'

Rising on his wings, Daedalus hovered, flying anxiously for love of his son. And just as a bird launches a tender fledgling from its lofty nest, Daedalus called to his son, schooling him in that fatal apprenticeship. The boy flapped his own wings, and took off into the air as Daedalus watched. And then, when satisfied, Daedalus set the course, his son following.

The boy flew as instructed at first, but then began to enjoy his flight too much as a boy will do, and left his guide and father's wisdom to roam the ranges of heaven. The scorching sun so close softened and melted the fragrant wax that bound his wings, leaving his arms bare. Calling to his father as he fell, the boy was swallowed by the blue sea.

Daedalus reached an idle shore and waited for his son. Seven days he stood by the shore, searching the constant swell, until the surf finally brought word of the boy's fate. On the waves Daedalus saw the many feathers of his craft. He sank into the sand and cursed himself and his gift, rubbing the gritty sand through his hair and across his face, mixing it with salty tears, as salty as the ocean itself.

When the tide had done its job, Daedalus pulled his son's body from the swell and buried it. Another seven days he sat motionless by the sea and the grave of his son, and named the blue sea and the island. And still today, the island keeps the name of Icaria.

*   *   *   *

They traveled down the mountain as Perseus told his tale, passing in and out of brilliant landscape, surreal against its dull counterpart. The journey took much longer than Perseus had thought, and it was late in the day when they came to the bottom of the mountain.

The trees thinned into an airy forest. Between the trees grew tall dry grass and an occasional thorny shrub with red, ovular berries. Small boulders dotted with mint green lichen were scattered between these. Just past one of the boulders, Perseus and Cyprian found a curious pathway. The flat, straight trail was littered with leaves and elevated from the rest of the ground. Though the pathway veered slightly southward, it seemed to be the easiest path, and they took it.

Soon the pathway descended into a slight depression in the land, a shallow bowl, in which a marsh formed on either side. The marshland was strangely beautiful; moss draped over the crooked trees, dying bushes and small boulders between them, all surrounded by swirling long grass, all set in a thin layer of water. Beyond the marsh on the right hand side, loomed a giant boulder field. Huge monoliths jutted from the ground and were stacked on top of each other till they were taller than the trees. Crannies of darkness filled the voids between, beneath, and through the rocks. It seemed a field of wonder, and tugged slightly on Perseus's desire—an adventure he would have undertaken in his youth. But they had no time to explore the field; the book was waiting.

As the boulder field fell behind, the path passed over a shallow creek on a small stone bridge. Appearing on the right was a mounded field of golden hue, shining in the strong sunlight. It did not have the sheen of the hybrid world, yet the gold was brilliant against the dull brown of the trees and the bright blue of the sky. The path then crossed another branch of the same creek, and in minutes the marsh waters lessened and the path rose to the lip of the forested bowl.

In the far distance was the ridge that held the runes, though the runes were blocked from view. The near landscape rolled, allowing for a majority of the land to be hidden in deep troughs, and was divided into two sections—green, sharply rolling hills to the left and golden brown gently rolling hills to the right.

Perseus and Cyprian followed the path, which skirted the green hills and remained in the woods, soon coming to the clearing of golden brown grasses, where the path ended facing west. Not far beyond the field the land sloped upward again, and the far ridge sat behind a closer crest of trees. A hundred yards to the right was a wooden fence, slats criss-crossing each other between vertical posts.

As Perseus and Cyprian started westward through the field, Perseus noticed the crop was wheat. His stomach cried out in want. Though it had been only half a day since he had eaten, he felt empty and weary. One look at Cyprian showed the young satyr was also tiring, struggling to take another step, continuing forward out of sheer will.

The wheat reminded Perseus of the Taenaran meadow, of the mill by the stream that might have been full of wheat, or flour; it was the right season. If only he had thought to bring flour along to make a loaf or two of bread. Or maybe if he had brought some of the meat filled leaves he would not feel so faint. To eat of Nemesis would be perverse, but it would also mean strength and life. Such was the way of the world. To live, one must eat.

"What's done is done," Perseus said, and forgave his regret. He halted in the middle of the field and began gathering the wheat. "Cyprian!"

"There are trees ahead," Cyprian yelled as he continued forward, left foot dragging heavily in the rich soil, more heavily than Perseus could ever remember. "Fruit trees."

Perseus paused from his labor and looked toward the distant trees. They were planted in neat rows, and although he could not tell what kind of trees they were, the copse was definitely an orchard.

Visible above the orchard were the runes, silhouetted against the sinking sun. It was a roofed platform with railing. Stairs descended from the platform before disappearing behind the orchard trees.

Definitely a tower, Perseus thought as he walked forward, toward the ready-made food, grabbing wheat stalks on his way. *Tomorrow we shall see it.*

Perseus arrived at the orchard and was delighted by the find. It was an apple orchard, full of short trees with smooth, healthy bark stretched over knotted trunks and arthritic branches. The leaves were dull green, but the fruit was luscious and full, almost bursting through the reddish-green skin.

Cyprian was already seated against one of the trees, a dozen apples in his lap. Sweet juice ran down his chin as he ate. Perseus spread his cloak on the ground and set the wheat he had been carrying in it before picking a few apples from the tree and sitting beside his friend, relieved to be off his aching feet.

The taste was heavenly sweetness, and Perseus ate as quickly as Cyprian. Only the brisk wind and contented lapping of mouth to fruit could be heard as the sun quickly descended. When the apples in their laps were gone they picked more and ate until their stomachs were relieved of emptiness. Then they lay still, looking through the orchard branches at the deepening blue sky.

"We camp here," Perseus announced. He grudgingly got to his feet and pulled his cloak next to the field. "But there is work to do before we rest. I need you to collect wheat, while I gather wood?"

Cyprian nodded and yawned.

"I'll be back shortly," Perseus said, and walked back through the field toward the forest.

Cyprian got to his feet, pulled the nearest stalks of wheat from their bed, and set them on Perseus's opened cloak with the others. His shoulders ached from carrying the pack, as did his legs, making him feel as if sleep would be fraught with discomfort. Yet his eyes drifted shut as he worked the methodical work.

Shortly, Perseus returned and started a small fire under the tree closest to the field. A circle of land brightly lit from the fire showed just how dark the sky had become.

"There will be much danger ahead," Perseus said gravely, starting the conversation delayed from the morning. He joined Cyprian in collecting wheat.

"Yes," Cyprian said.

"You still choose to continue?"

Cyprian's eyes livened. "You don't want me to come," he said.

"It's your path to choose, if you wish it," Perseus said, pausing from the labor. "But you know little of the quest's purpose or the danger you face. It is time you understood that which you have fallen into." Cyprian said nothing, stared at the ground. "Have you heard of the book of Antioch?"

"Yes."

"Then you know of it as legend?"

Cyprian shook his head and looked up at Perseus. "Niobe taught me of the book as an important artifact from the old world."

"Then you are smarter than I," Perseus said kindly, and Cyprian smiled.

"She said it was the fruit of the world, from which springs all life and death, and that it was protected by most powerful spirits of the old world."

"True indeed, my friend. The book *was* protected by powerful spirits, the oracles of legend. And in the very meadow at the base of Taenarus. That is how I came to be the owner of this quest. I am the rider from the east.

"I had been sent by my father in search of guidance from an oracle about the threat of war from Phrygia. The journey from Larissa to Delphi was supposed to take less than a month, and was supposed to be my introduction to the southern cities of Thessaly. All was well through the first stage, traveling through Pharae then Phylace and on through Trachis. I met aristocrats and friends of my father, attended many feasts and balls, met many young ladies.

"I aquaintanced myself well where I went, and left Trachis, the last of my stops, after the second week out, neither dawdling nor hurrying. On the hills above Delphi, I passed riders who warned me of destruction in the south. I feared the Phrygians had already come, and hastened my pace, riding hard into Delphi.

"With morning's light, I found the city in ruins. Weary, Nemesis and I rested in the shade of the ruined fountain of Kassotis. There, a band of ruffians in dragon-crested gear ambushed me, and I fought bravely through their ranks, slaying all who did not flee from my wrath. I would have tracked down the remaining cowards but for the need of an oracle's wisdom. There was more at stake than Delphi. So I fled and proceeded to Athens. The nearly normal state of the city gave me hope that Delphi's ruin was an anomaly, a case of ruffians ransacking poorly defended cities. In better spirits, I procured a small ship and sailed to Delos.

"However, before reaching shore, I could tell the island ruined. Great plumes of smoke towered high into the air, and beneath them fires raged across the wide landscape. I landed on the lofty shore anyway and scouted the land. Not a soul was left.

"On the shore I remained, and prayed for guidance. When, on the third day, none had come, I resolved to return to Thessaly. Not three hours on the water, however, a great storm blew in from the south and battered my ship to pieces. Alone, afloat on a wooden chest, I washed up on the island of Seriphos."

Perseus paused from his tale, was drawn from it by memories of deep hurt, the cause unremembered, and looked toward Thaeron, averting Cyprian's gaze. After a brief moment, he continued.

"But indeed that tale is for another day, dear Cyprian. For now you only need know that after more than two years since washing up on Seriphos I made my way to war-torn Argolis. After countless battles with gruff barbarians, and after countless days without sleep I was set upon by a cursed Giant, loosed from Arima, and dealt a blow that sent me into darkness. Only by the grace of Nemesis did I escape death.

"It was the cottage in the Taenaran meadow, in which I awoke, under the care of Sarah and Malachai, the last two true oracles. There I was nursed to life and learned of my fate entwined in that of the Book of Antioch. It had been stolen from the spring beside the cottage."

"That spring feeds the Taenaran River," Cyprian said.

"So it does," Perseus replied. "It was also a gateway between our world and this one. The book was hidden there and guarded by the oracles from those who sought it. However, their powers could not touch a young boy in this world, a young boy who stumbled upon the sacred pool and the book, and took it for his own.

"On the way to the lights of Thaeron, in search of treasure, the boy, his friend, and the book fell into the hands of a *drakamor*. That, Cyprian, is why the world began to change. That is why the cottage lights appeared. That is why seven dawns arose in the course of twenty years. If the book is not returned to safe hands, and to its original, the world will continue toward chaos; it will move into darkness. Such is my quest. To find the book and return it to safety."

Perseus fell silent and plucked a handful of wheat. The swishing of the grains was the only accompaniment to Cyprian's thoughts, and his. Perseus had been unwittingly forced into this quest, and was only now coming to grips with it. It was as things were, and it was as things were meant to be. What he was unsure of was Cyprian's part.

"I wish to come," Cyprian whispered, almost too quietly to be heard.

"You must be sure, Cyprian. The decision is not to be taken lightly."

"Please," Cyprian replied.

"It is said that to face a *drakamor* is worse than death," Perseus said, and then closed his eyes, brought to mind an old children's rhyme his father had taught him—one that now seemed too ruthless to speak to a child. "To know of life is not enough, to enter the house of a *drakamor*, you must know of sorrow and of death, and also evils long before, else your lifeblood seek the earth, and soulless enter Hades door." There was more to the rhyme that Perseus did not speak. Much more, though he judged this enough to scare Cyprian. "This is but a taste of what awaits us."

"I wish to come," Cyprian said on the verge of tears.

"I cannot promise you will keep your life or soul, or I mine when all is done."

"Please, don't send me away," Cyprian whispered, tears coming to his eyes, running down his rosy cheeks. "P…p…lease."

Perseus sighed, gathered a quivering Cyprian in his arms, and hugged him. "I'll not send you away," he said.

"Please….I wish to come."

Perseus again looked toward Thaeron. The dark mountain commanded the skyline and seemed to draw Perseus's eyes to it. It was smaller than Taenarus, yet looked similar. The two were bound to each other somehow, connected through a maze of darkness and forces beyond Perseus's comprehension. The same could be true, Perseus thought, of him and Cyprian. How had it chanced that Cyprian stole his bow, and was slow enough to be caught? How had it chanced that Cyprian saved him from the wraith on Taenarus, and then chose to brave the underworld?

Cyprian's fate was clearly entwined with his and the book. Such a young boy though. But a boy with a stout heart. The Fates had been kind to choose such a companion for Perseus.

"It is the two of us who continue, and I am thankful for that."

"R…eally?" Cyprian asked, the tears drying almost as quickly as they had come.

"I swear it on the Styx," Perseus said. "I had thought the quest mine and mine alone. Yet I see you are bound to it for your part. Tomorrow we continue west."

"Tomorrow we continue," Cyprian said bravely. And with the words and their tone, Perseus knew that Cyprian belonged to the quest, for good or for bad.

"It has been a trying day for you," Perseus said. "I'll finish with the wheat."

Cyprian tried to shake his head in protest, but exhaustion took hold of his mind, and he nodded in agreement. He lay next to the fire, watching through half-closed eyes as Perseus plucked stalks and pounded them onto his cloak, removing the grains. Soon though, Cyprian's eyes were closed, and he only heard the rhythmic thumping of stalk against cloak.

When the sound ended, the change awoke Cyprian. He forced his eyes open and saw Perseus shaking the grains into the pack. Perseus then put a branch on the fire and lay beside Cyprian, covering both of them with the cloak.

*   *   *   *

Perseus remained awake, listening to the satyr's calmed breathing as he thought about the old rhyme. He had dredged it up from a childhood that was filled with much happiness. But in the happiness were these rhymes that his father had taught him, that fascinated him and filled him with wanderlust. They had never kept him from the forest like they had his sister, who often refused to leave the palace for fear of evil spirits. And Perseus teased her endlessly about her fear of creatures long since departed from the earth.

Now, he knew it was not so. And the rhyme seemed much more than a story to keep children from wandering too far from home. The rhyme seemed an enigma of words, a riddle to be thought upon. And so Perseus thought upon it, tracing the lines, as his mind raced toward sleep. Not the lines he had learned from his father, but the lines he found in a curious text during his studies in Byblis.

He could see the ancient text in front of him, could smell the musty cover that was cracked and falling apart. And inside, the parchment was stained and often missing. But that endeared the book to Perseus all the more. He always sat in a far corner of the tower room, away from other eyes.

The memory of it felt right. He had not thought of the book once since leaving Byblis, but now he could see it clearly. It was as if the memory had been buried for a reason, hidden until it was needed. He could see the exact page. The one poem surrounded by a sketch of two pillars with snakes twining up them, the words, delicately crafted and beautiful, as beautiful as the night sky during May Fair.

So it was that the ancient verse traced through Perseus's mind as he lay beneath a fruitful apple tree.

> *The merk of lyf is but a remnaunt part,*
> *To fighte the blak of the drakamor herte,*
> *Yow must knowen of sorwe and eek of deeth,*
> *And brethe the malefice in evil's foule breeth,*
> *Er yow seken the greet spirit of olde,*
> *Else your redde lyfblood wol meet the grounde cold,*

And sauns your soule enter Hades derk door.
To knowen of tyme never the moore,
But fro deeths grace cometh hir lyf divine,
Softe and smal, the weed grewen whan it shynes
Tere the vertue fro the deedly temple whyte,
Whyte falles to blakness and hath no moore byt
And wikke wyle falles into shaplesse drafs[14]

The riddle was still in Perseus's mind when he smelled the slight change in the air, and knew that tomorrow would be miserable. He moved the pack underneath the cloak and put another branch on the fire. The heat radiated outward nicely, and gave Perseus warm thoughts to blot out the pending rain.

*   *   *   *

The rain started in the early morning, cold and misty, and soaked through the protective cloak around Cyprian and Perseus, chilling their bodies, waking them in unpleasant twilight. Muscles stiff, the two unwrapped themselves from the cloak and stood. As they stretched, their teeth began to chatter, causing them to shorten their stretch, pick up their things, and begin walking.

On the way through the orchard, they picked apples from the trees and ate of them. The fruit was unpleasantly cold and wet and tasted of nothing. Hardly the glorified feast of last night. Yet it filled their stomachs as well as any meal, Perseus thought, as he picked more apples to fill the pack on Cyprian's shoulders.

They crested the orchard hillock and saw nothing of the far tree line or the ruins. The view was blocked by a thick white fog that lingered over the land beyond the end of the orchard, which was marked by a road. But the road was like none Perseus had ever seen. The closest thing he could compare it to was the great road in Larissa. This road, however, was not cobbles and sand; it was seamless and without cracks or fissures or missing stone through which a horse could break its leg.

As they neared the road, Cyprian's hand took hold of Perseus's sword strap. His eyes darted left, along with his head. Then he pulled closer to Perseus, clung to him, frightened. And that's when Perseus heard the rumbling.

It was familiar to him—from his vision of this world in the oracle's cottage. Except the vision had been more than watching events from the outside. The experience had been more visceral. Perseus had smelled what David had smelled, seen what David had seen, experienced what David had experienced, thought what David had thought. For those moments, he had been David. And this rumbling sound, according to what Perseus remembered, was normal.

"Don't worry," Perseus said. "It is only a...bus." Except what passed through the narrow strip of trees was blue and smaller than the bus in the vision. Perseus shrugged. "I have seen bigger."

There were no more busses on the road as Perseus and Cyprian neared and crossed, and walked into the fog that loomed over another field. The rain intensified, and large drops pelted Perseus's eyes every time he looked forward, trying to keep his bearings. From last night's camp the tower had been directly west of them. However, once they crossed the road and entered the fog, it became impossible to tell which direction they were heading.

They found the tree line without problem, and entered it quickly for the little protection it gave; the high branches impeded the rain, and the fog was somewhat disbursed. Perseus judged where he thought the tower was and turned left.

Less than a hundred yards away they found the tower amidst the cluttered tree line. Surrounding its base were short walls of small, rounded stone dotted with lichen. The tower itself had four corner supports, which were connected by trusses. Inside the structure were sets of stairs and landings that went from support to support as they rose toward the platform.

Although the tower was mostly metal covered with a pale green paint, there were portions tainted by Perseus and Cyprian's world, where the metal seamlessly melded into richly grained wood splotched with bright green moss.

Cyprian and Perseus laid out their drenched belongings beneath the tower, sat on a dry stone, and huddled inside Perseus cloak for warmth. Neither felt much like talking, and once their heat mixed together and was trapped sleep began to call. Perseus eyes drooped shut. When they opened, seemingly seconds later, the rain had slowed to a drizzle and the gray haze had lightened, the fog lifted.

"Come, Cyprian," Perseus said groggily, stirring the satyr from his nap. "We should scout the land while we can."

Perseus stood and started up the stairs, checking each for decay, especially those that were both metal and wood. Cyprian followed. The higher they climbed the more wood replaced metal, and Perseus walked slower, treading lightly on each step before putting his full weight on it.

"I don't like this," Cyprian said. "Though I have liked very little since the Alluvian crags. When is it I shall get to enjoy my surroundings with you?"

Perseus laughed and patted Cyprian's head. "I don't know, my young friend. Maybe not for some time."

"Maybe not," Cyprian said and smiled, though he only half meant it. "Though, I would like to see such a day."

"As would I," Perseus said.

The last flight of stairs saw no more metal, only mossy wood. These stairs were as sturdy as the others and when Perseus arrived at the platform he offered Cyprian first passage onto the tower's lookout.

It was a small area, covered by a roof and enclosed by a solid wall that rose just above Cyprian's head. He pulled his head over the railing and, looking westward, saw more tracts of farmland broken up by slim lines of trees and an occasional forest. The farmland was mostly lush pasture, empty lush pasture.

Many small, indistinguishable hills were visible in the distance, before which lay a creek, running in and out of woods and pasture, swollen with the morning's rain. The water was brown and sick, and fallen trees bobbed in the swift current. Spanning the creek was a red covered bridge, which connected a dirty, muddy, and deeply rutted roadway. On the opposite side of the creek, the roadway turned north and disappeared behind a line of trees. On the near side of the creek, the roadway led toward Thaeron, passing the tower on the right. He and Perseus must have paralleled it since leaving the orchard.

"Look at this," Perseus said.

"Huh?"

"The land. We are headed directly into the joining of the worlds."

Cyprian walked over to the opposite side of the tower, and pulled himself above the railing. The fog had thinned extensively, allowing him to see the field and orchard. Behind that was Thaeron, which looked small to Cyprian, no more than a mere hill now that he was not on it. And to the left of Thaeron was a shorter hill, barren, rocks strewn down the face, golden grass sticking out from between the rocks. But as far as Cyprian could see, there was no change in brilliance.

"I don't understand," he said.

Perseus lifted Cyprian onto his shoulders. "What we just came from was mostly this world, untouched," Perseus said, and pointed out small patches of isolated radiance. The patches were all on Thaeron and spread across a wide area. "We must have wandered unwittingly back and forth to hit most of those patches on our decent," Perseus continued. "The tower's change from metal to wood. And the roadway…"

To Cyprian's left was the roadway they paralleled. West of the tower it was dirt. East of the tower, however, the road was seamless stone. Perseus slowly turned around. It was then that Cyprian noticed how the land traveled from lackluster to bright. Even the air and droplets of rain rippled with an unnatural light. Perseus stopped turning when they were looking west.

"The two worlds are completely joined on this side, and that troubles me. It troubles me immensely."

"We must go on," Cyprian said, the statement quavering, bordering on being a question; but it was a statement.

"We must go on," Perseus agreed and put Cyprian back to the ground. "But we must be extremely careful. From now on we know nothing of the dangers on our path. The woodland creatures may be twisted hybrids of both worlds, and that could prove more perilous than anything you or I have ever encountered."

As Perseus fell silent and stared out at the land, Cyprian pulled himself up to the railing and looked with him, glazing over the meaningless features, the covered bridge. Suddenly, his arms weakened and he felt nauseated. He dropped from the railing, crumpled to the floor, and lay still, unable to feel his body. Intense heat swept through his consciousness and his eyes rolled backwards.

White lights exploded, faded into a remembrance. Cyprian was falling through the black surface that separated the underworld from the mortal world. Although he had not awakened for some time, he could feel Perseus beside him, and then Perseus gone. Perseus had left, and that's why Cyprian was alone. Perseus had left, only returning after Cyprian awoke and called.

The vision faded, was replaced by light. And then, Cyprian felt his eyes roll forward and the heat recede, and he was aware that Perseus was next to him, cradling his head and speaking for him to wake. Cyprian opened his eyes and found Perseus's face drawn into confusion, his mouth speaking of concern. The words gave Cyprian little comfort, however. He had just remembered. Not something that had actually happened in the underworld, and not something physical, but he remembered a feeling. And the remembered feeling wasn't from the past; it was from the future. Perseus was going to leave him.

"You're going to leave me," he said coldly.

Perseus recoiled, though his eyes showed relief, quickly changing to confusion. He knelt quietly, pondering the statement and the cruel certainty with which it had been delivered. And the circumstances with which it had been delivered. After Cyprian had collapsed, Perseus had had just enough time to put a comforting hand behind his head before the satyr's eyes fluttered open, white as a dove, a heartbeat later rolling forward.

Perseus was unmistaken in what he had just witnessed. "You have the gift," he said in awe of the gift, bemused by what it spoke.

"What?" Cyprian said curtly.

"You have the gift of foresight."

"Yes. No. I don't know." Cyprian sat up, his anger deflecting into hurt. He no longer remembered anything from the vision except for the overwhelming feeling of abandonment. "You're going to leave me."

Perseus sat pensively for a moment before standing and looking at the view beyond the tower once more. "I'll not tell you it won't happen," he finally said. "Prophecies are powerful things. But you must know that if that happens, if we are separated, it will not be by my choice. If there were something I could say to make you believe that, I would. Our paths have already been chosen for us. Where they cross and where they diverge, I have no control."

Cyprian sat for a long time, and Perseus let him be while he calculated their route through the landscape to the house of the *drakamor*. At last, there was movement behind him.

"I don't want it to happen," Cyprian said quietly, stepping beside Perseus.

"Nor do I. Nor does anyone who would have to make such a decision, if it is a decision at all."

"But why?" Cyprian asked. "Why does it have to happen?"

"I don't know," Perseus said. "All I can tell you is that the Book of Antioch must be retrieved. And to retrieve it, perhaps we must part. It is the book we seek at all cost, not companionship. That is the best I can answer." Perseus fell quiet for a moment, then asked, "You didn't see how this would come about?"

"No," Cyprian said.

"Then it may be death that delivers me from you," he said gravely. The words lingered in the air before passing away. "If that is the case, then you must continue. You must retrieve the book and find a way to keep it safe."

"But—"

"No buts," Perseus said gently but sternly. "If it is the Fate's will, that is the way it will be."

Cyprian looked desperately at Perseus, searching, hoping for another answer. Hundreds of scenarios flooded his head, interrupted his ability to think. He had spent countless nights alone in the Taenaran forest, but this was an entirely different world, one that even Perseus was wary of. What would come of a small satyr in a hybrid world filled with evil? He did not want to go on alone should it come to that.

Cyprian sighed and released a fit of tears...*the will of the fates*...tears that caused him to feel empty inside...*at all cost*...and torn; he would be alone, again. He had always survived alone, but he didn't want to...*the way it will be*...he wanted companionship.

But it didn't matter what he wanted. It never did. And it never would. He was a pawn to destiny as was everyone else. Perseus was right. The book was the important thing, the only thing that mattered.

Cyprian nodded in acquiescence, choking back his remaining tears. His head hurt, and he felt loneliness as if it were already upon him.

"I couldn't have asked for a braver companion," Perseus said and put a comforting hand on Cyprian's shoulder. Through the loneliness, Cyprian felt happiness trying to break through. He found the brightness and clung to it with everything he could muster.

"Thank you."

"If you wish it, we will stay here for the night and keep dry. However, I feel as if we should continue as soon as we might. There is no telling what a delay might cause."

Cyprian swallowed and nodded "Then we go."

"Glad to hear it," Perseus said, though he was not sure he was. He helped Cyprian up onto the railing and pointed to a nondescript hill in the distance, northwest of the tower. "We are headed there." He then swung his finger back to the west. "Yet we cross the river on that covered bridge."

Cyprian had followed Perseus finger, though he was unable to tell which hill he had been pointing at. He could, however, see the bridge clearly. The river had risen in the few moments since he had last looked, and was close to the bridge's bottom. Waves, bigger than they should have been, leapt from the river it seemed and splashed into the support beams.

Perseus's gaze returned to the nondescript hill. "Without trouble," he said, trying not to accent the words, failing, "we should be there by dark." He untied the strap that held his knife to his belt, knowing that Cyprian's prophecy would come true, one way or the other. Regardless, Perseus continued speaking as if they would arrive together. "But we will wait until morning, and the strength of day to face the *drakamor*. Blessed be the sun on a day of death." Perseus held the knife out to Cyprian. "Should we split, you will need protection. If you reach the house without me, wait until dawn. If I do not come, it's up to you."

Cyprian took the small, unadorned knife and looked at it briefly while he worked a lump out of his throat. "It shall be done," he said at last, and tied the cord of the knife's sheath around his waist.

Lightning crashed down from the sky for the first time, signaling a change in the storm. The bolt fell upon a distant tree and immediately fire and smoke rose from the timber. A second later, a voluminous rally of thunder roared in approval, bringing with it another onslaught of hard rain.

"We'd better get moving," Perseus said, "before the Furies release ice from the sky as well."

PARTING[15]

They collected their belongings under volleys of thunder and lightning, and regretfully left the tower's shelter. Rain dripped through the canopy, slopping the ground, turning the rocks and roots slippery. Perseus slipped almost every step; Cyprian faired slightly better, slipping every other step.

Through the small band of trees and over a wooden fence brought them to a pasture. Perseus stepped into the ankle high grass, found it soggy and difficult. His foot sunk into the earth and settled ankle deep. A powerful spell of wind drove the rain down harder. Perseus took a few more steps into the field and found his knees buried underneath the sludge. Cyprian was buried up to his thighs.

"It's impossible," Perseus yelled over the rumbling thunder. "We must make for the road along the edge of the forest."

He took the pack from Cyprian and slung it over a shoulder as they turned back to the woods. Once at the fencerow they skirted the field, using the fence to keep from sinking into the mud. Once at the road, Perseus returned the pack to Cyprian and began walking down the hill, sheltering his face from the driving rain.

The sky crackled, and lightning landed in the pasture to Perseus right, behind a stand of trees that would have been perfect shelter for animals had there been any. Almost immediately, another streak of lightning flew from the sky, landing not twenty feet from the first. But when this strike landed, it did not dissipate; the bluish-white torrent spread out like water poured onto a flat stone. As quickly as the energy spread it dissipated, lost to the ground.

At the same time, Perseus slipped in the mud and landed on his back. He lay for a moment, wondering what this new lightning meant, if it meant anything. There was no way to tell, and he picked himself up to continue walking, head down to avoid the rain. At the bottom of the hill, he bumped into an unmoving Cyprian, whose gaze was held to the right.

"What is it?" Perseus asked, as he followed the satyr's head.

A section of the wooden fencing beyond the road was decimated, splintered, bits of railing strewn in muddy puddles. Three massive black cows lay close to the broken fencing, blood running from their trampled, broken hides, mixing with the rain, washing away. The animals were larger than Perseus had ever seen.

One cow lay still, railing running through its soft belly and udder. The other two cows twitched spastically. Both animal's faces had been crushed, the place between their eyes concave and soft, wavering loosely every time they breathed a muted sound of impending death.

It was this that Cyprian was looking at, yet there was more. A sloppy path of dark earth was carved into the green pasture and led downhill from the fence. It followed along the edge of a steep hill inside the pasture, keeping to the low grounds, passing out of sight. From this unknown, came muffled mooing and stomping, a quiet sound on the soft earth. Minute vibration shook the road, as if the ground was splitting open somewhere distant.

"Something powerful," Cyprian said.

"Yes," Perseus said. "I can feel it."

Slowly, tentatively, they walked farther along the road, bringing into view a section of pasture hidden by the steep hill. At first they saw the fringe of the large herd; the animals swayed into view, moving as a group, and then swayed back disappearing behind the hill. The mooing grew louder; the rumbling strengthened.

When the entire gully was visible, Perseus and Cyprian stopped, stood at the edge of the road watching the odd sight. There were hundreds, perhaps a thousand cows huddled together in a rough circle, facing inward. In a small opening in the center of the herds were two bulls, dancing a menacing dance, circling each other, hooves pawing the ground anxiously, heads bobbing erratically, needle-sharp horns cutting the air; their eyes were aflame, their large nostrils snorting fiery winds. One bull was marbled black and white; the other bull completely black, bigger than the first.

"Dear Phoebus." Perseus sighed, instinctively reaching for his bow. His hand searched his back for the ash staff before realizing it was not there; it had been gone since Taenarus. In its stead, Perseus loosened the sword in its scabbard. "If they stampede," he told Cyprian, "run to the nearest tree and climb."

"And what of you?"

"I'll do the same," he said, and then added absently, "we should not be seeing this."

"Then let us go."

The tension in the pasture grew and made Perseus uneasy; he wanted to walk away. Yet, the mass moved with grace, the bulls in the middle continuously circling, and he stood transfixed by this thing of monstrous beauty.

"Not yet," he said.

Lightning erupted from the sky, hitting the ground atop the pasture's hill. The after-glow surged from the strike, traveled down the hill, and flowed into the circle of animals. Atop the hill, a lone tree burned. The cows swayed faster, hooves pounding louder, plunging to and fro in the soft mud. The lightning torrent spread and diminished, returned to the earth. As if on cue, the black bull reared up on its hind legs.

He lunged toward the other in a powerful movement, horns aiming for a fatal blow. The spotted bull dodged the attack by stepping to the right, and at the same time moved in. With a flick of its head, the spotted bull sent a fated horn into the shoulder of his foe, drawing first blood. The black beast bellowed ferociously, and spun to face the other. Again they circled.

The cows furthest from the action, on the perimeter of the circle, pranced restlessly. Some put their forelegs on those in front of them, attempting to climb on top. Others pushed inward, getting nowhere, but closing the inner circle. As a mass, the cows swayed backward, catching the eager ones on the outskirts off balance, crushing them beneath angry hooves.

The spotted bull lunged, missed, and backed away before the other could take advantage. Again they circled. Again one lunged. And so the cycle continued, each bull slashing, missing, then connecting, until both sets of horns were coated in blood.

Thunder roared throughout the sky and died. A moment of stillness followed releasing Perseus from his daze.

"Let's go," Cyprian said uneasily, tugging on Perseus's sleeve.

Before Perseus could respond, an almost invisible streak of lightning flew from the clouds into the mass of cattle. A thick, acrid smoke rose from where the lightning had struck, sending a sickeningly pungent smell into the air. The herds flew into chaos. The open space between the bulls filled, and two sets of horns slashed wildly, bringing up chunks of severed cow. Horrified bellows filled the air

"Yes," Perseus replied, backing up with Cyprian's tug. "Yes, you are right. We should go."

*   *   *   *

The bellows muted under the sound of gushing water from a river that was yet to be seen. Woods filled in beside the road, which started up a small rise. The trees grew tangled and dense, encroached on the road in threatening measures. The road curved ahead and with it went the trees, whose branches stretched across it, high above, filtering the cloud-diminished light even further. It was not yet mid-day, but it seemed twilight or later.

One last bellow reached through the forest, and then all sound fell quiet to the water's fury. Weeds filled in between the trees, and emptiness filled the cracks between these. Nothing stirred from the forest depths, yet it felt as if something might at any moment.

Unconsciously, Cyprian moved closer to Perseus. As they crested the slight rise and walked around a long bend, he nervously glanced about, looking for movement. The forest remained as it was, damp and dull; the silence, the stillness mocked Cyprian's unease, and he felt a mounting rush of fear that eventually broke from his mouth.

"Come out," he said, spinning around, waving his knife in the air.

The forest did not answer.

Cyprian laughed nervously, frightfully, but he felt better. And when the bend was finally put behind, he saw that two hundred yards ahead the trees drew back from the road; a slim band of grass grew in their stead. The grass was a welcome sight, and would have lightened Cyprian's hope even further had the bridge not been just beyond.

The road narrowed to the width of the bridge, which was set high above the swollen river. Waves were not crashing against the red siding as Cyprian had thought at the tower. Yet he wondered if it had been a trick of the mind or a trick of some devilry.

Half the distance to the bridge the ground began to quake, growing from a dim rumble to a low growl. Cyprian regretted yelling at the forest. Whatever had been dormant was awake.

The quaking grew louder. The forest remained still. And as Cyprian whirled about to face the evil, knife ready to slash, he felt the rumbling coming from behind, not from the forest. He spun to the source and saw a blinding mass of black stampeding toward him, the sound hidden by the water's roar.

"The herd," Cyprian yelled. But by then Perseus had felt the ground too, and had seen the herd, under fifty yards away.

"To the trees," Perseus yelled, though he could not hear his own voice.

Cyprian's hooves caught easily in the mud, and in five quick steps he was safely behind a large tree, Perseus a moment behind.

The black bull led the herd. Blood drooled from his mouth and nose, covered his horns, ran from tiny slashes in his flanks. The bull and herd passed without slowing. The trampling hooves, combined with the river's wrath, made anything impossible to hear. The trees shook as violently as the ground. Cyprian mimed climbing the tree, but Perseus shook his head, knowing the cows would not stop their stampede to weave into the forest.

It seemed an eternity until the entire herd had passed and Perseus dared to walk onto the road. Most of the herd thundered across the wooden planks and disappeared into the distance. However, those on the outside of the mass were forced into the river where the road narrowed, and were swallowed by the swift current.

"Fates be with us," Perseus said quietly.

Cyprian nodded, and they began walking. A biting wind grew, sweeping through the road's corridor without sympathy. The rain stung as never before, leaving welts on Cyprian's bare chest. Perseus unfastened his cloak and wrapped it around the satyr's shoulders, tucking the long end into the straps of the bag.

"Thank you," Cyprian said.

Perseus nodded, then immediately tensed as a hollow boom came from the bridge. The sound quickly faded on the wind. Twice more the boom came from the bridge, twice disappearing behind them. Then it was no more.

*   *   *   *

The road ended at a stone ramp-way, on which the covered bridge sat precariously. The two support timbers that spanned the length of the river were weak and cracking. Yet, they looked strong enough to hold two small travelers. The roof peaked in the middle and sloped outward to the exterior walls, which were painted red. The shimmering rain pounded the paint, coated it with freshness, reminding Perseus of blood. On the inside of the bridge, the walls were flecked with scraps of flesh.

A trampled cow with three legs lay inside the structure, to the left side near the middle. Next to the cow, a large jagged hole was surrounded by thick, dark blood.

Beyond the short span of darkness, the road turned upstream, and was hidden behind a thin section of woods. Downstream, the woods continued thick and deep. Visible through the bridge was an open field trampled down by the cows.

Perseus looked at the bridge, the shelter that would keep him and Cyprian dry. Yet they remained in the rain, listening for the noise they had heard as they approached.

"It may have been the wood settling," Perseus said, doubtful.

There was something wrong. The water was too still, or too quiet. And the bridge was too silent for the amount of weight it has just borne. Creaking would be comforting, especially since the bridge was near to ruin. But there was none. There had only been the two thuds.

"What about another crossing," Cyprian suggested.

"There is no other. The river is swollen, the current swift."

"We could wait till the rain passes," Cyprian offered.

"We could," Perseus said. "But my heart tells me we press on."

The words echoed in Cyprian's mind, reminding him of the walls in the underworld. They echoed and then multiplied. He willed the voices away and allowed the water's roar to fill his mind instead. He looked past the foundation to the water. It had risen.

"If we must," he said, then shrugged off the rain and took a step onto the wooden planks.

"Stay on the right, and be quick," Perseus said, following, drawing his sword.

As Cyprian walked the river rose unnaturally, swelling upward, not outward, rising toward the height of the bridge. This Cyprian saw through the hole in the middle, and he quickened his pace. He had just passed the mutilated cow when a powerful force slammed against the bottom of the bridge, sending a hollow boom through the now swaying enclosure.

"Run!" Perseus yelled as another jolt hit the bridge.

This time the floorboards groaned fiercely and gave way, sending a shower of splinters into the air that hit Cyprian in the back. The bridge heaved upward, then crashed back down, knocking Cyprian off his feet. The timbers groaned violently, mixing with an unnatural roar that echoed both human and river. Above the din a clear ringing resounded, and Cyprian was sure that Perseus had swung his sword.

The bridge shook heavily as Cyprian scampered to the stone ramp, into the light and rain. He turned, and saw the cause of Perseus's attack.

Surging through a giant hole in the floorboards, grappling with Perseus, was a massive form forged from the dirty river. The form was nearly eight feet tall, a pillar of water up to its waist, where it took the form of a man. Two curved horns protruded from its brow.

The river demon swung its thick arms at Perseus, aiming for his head. Perseus dodged the menacing blow as he fought to keep his balance on the writhing floorboards. The demon swung again, and Perseus brought the blade up. The demon's arm passed through the steel with little resistance, and formless water crashed down on Perseus's head. A hollow roar filled the bridge as the water harmlessly drained through the floorboards. The demon drew new life from the river and another arm grew, as perfect as the first.

"Go," Perseus yelled as he dove toward Cyprian, avoiding another powerful swipe. He rolled and was quickly on his feet dodging another attack.

Cyprian was paralyzed and could will himself to flee no more than he could to fly. He watched the demon block Perseus from the near shore. And with each attack, Perseus was driven backward, avoided a swiping arm by diving and swinging his sword at the same time. The demon howled as his fingers fell away; but within seconds there were new fingers, and the demon dove for Perseus, came up short, liquefied. The harmless water poured through the cracks in the floorboards. A moment of stillness filled Cyprian with a brief glimmer of hope.

Perseus was on his feet and running when another forceful jolt slammed into the bridge's undercarriage, directly in front of Cyprian. Perseus staggered, but kept his balance. Again the jolt came, and Perseus braced himself against the wall.

"Cyprian, go!" he yelled, followed by one last ungodly boom.

The old wood twisted and cracked, screamed in agony, as one of the support beams broke loose from the foundation. Stone pelted Cyprian's face, and he was momentarily blinded. The bridge twisted and writhed, and the other support beam bent with tremendous will, dropping the bridge closer to the water, opening a gap between the foundation and bridge.

Through the gap the demon rose. It grabbed the bridge in its massive hold and shook it violently. A support beam snapped in half; the middle of the bridge sagged further, dipping into the rushing water.

The demon heaved one final time, removing the last support beam from the stone foundation, loosing the wood into the river's rage. On the other side of the stream, the beams slid easily from the foundation, and the entire bridge plunged into the current and was carried downstream. The demon disappeared into the murky water.

Cyprian threw off the cloak and pack, keeping a hold on his knife, and raced into the woods, following the bridge as fast as he could. However, the woods were dense and the river fast, and the gap between Cyprian and the bridge increased. He heard a lone cry from Perseus, an agonized cry, and fought through the thickening brambles with a will of iron.

"Perseus!" he yelled.

A vine twined around his leg, caught him suddenly, jerking Cyprian to the ground. He desperately tried to free his foot, yet it seemed that the vine tightened as he resisted, tightening and choking as the bridge sank into the water and vanished beneath the waves.

"Perseus," he cried, standing, thrashing his captive leg. The vine noticeably tightened, dug into Cyprian's flesh. Cyprian swore and violently cut the vine away. He slashed a path through the brambles to the edge of the river, hoping to see the bridge in the distance. There was nothing. The river seemed calm. The rain had lessened.

*   *   *   *

Hot tears mixed with cold rain as Cyprian walked back to the road. He sat on the foundation and cried, watched the blurry brown water carry trees and branches downstream as quickly as it had carried Perseus.

A fresh bout of tears came and went. The rain continued, and soon Cyprian began to shiver. He didn't want to move; yet he knew he could not stay.

*Death delivers me…*he heard Perseus's voice speaking, did not wish to hear the rest. It came regardless.…*you must continue.*

Cyprian hit the ground with his tiny fist, sending a chilled ache into his hand. He didn't want to keep going. He wished he hadn't been so cold to Perseus. He wished the Fates would die. He wished he were back home where the rain wasn't so cold. He wished a million things, none of which would happen.

Cyprian donned the cloak and pulled his arms around his chest, trying to keep warm. Coldness seeped through the cloak and Cyprian shivered harder. Still he sat.

It wasn't until his teeth started chattering and his body was shaking convulsively that he stood on frigid legs. His face was numb; his hands were stiff and difficult to move; his knees ached with every movement. Yet he stood and began walking. Not out of a will to continue the quest, but out of a will to live.

Step after weary step, he trudged down the dirt road that passed between the edge of the field and the edge of the forest, wishing to think of nothing, forced to hear Perseus's last cry again and again.

TROUBLABLE DREEMS[16]

Cyprian didn't care where the road went; he only followed it out of ease, barely paying attention to the surroundings. His twisted foot ached for the first time since climbing Taenarus with Perseus, and Cyprian began to limp. He pulled the cloak tighter around his body, and soon stopped shivering. When the rain finally quit and the wind died down, pain like needles grew in Cyprian's fingers. After a long while it receded into warmth, and he was glad for the small comfort.

The road ran parallel to the river for a mile before turning away and heading west. The river's roar lessened to Cyprian's ear, leaving Perseus's cry as the lone sound in his head. The anguished cry played over and over, distorting each time; the anguish grew louder, sharper; it was filled with death. Perseus was dead. Cyprian could see Perseus's frightened face—the last face Perseus had made before the bridge plunged into the river. Perseus was gone; Cyprian was alone.

Trees grudgingly came and went along both sides of the road, and were replaced by field, pasture, fence, brush, and then more trees. Everything Cyprian passed looked ugly and desolate and worsened his mood. But when he was beneath the gloom of the overhanging branches he felt worst. The boughs swayed and rustled in light sweeping movements, whispering about Cyprian, laughing at him, mocking him. He hung his head and ignored the taunting, as he had done his entire life, until the trees were left behind.

After exiting one such stretch, Cyprian came upon a meadow, dotted with gray rocks, in which he saw something peculiar. A wispy light fluttering between a pair of rocks caught his attention and brought momentary peace. As quickly as the light had appeared, though, it vanished.

But for the first time Cyprian looked around the foreign world and noticed its beauty. And he felt pity. Pity for himself. Pity for Perseus. Pity for the world as it was; the grass, minty green and shimmering with the sweetened rain; the grand trees, both ancient and young; the crisp air, fragrant with the changing season; the rocks; the rich earth; the harvest crops.

And pity for the light. Cyprian knew he had seen it, more by the fact that he had felt it, could still feel it. If the book were not found, the light and all of nature would change.

But Perseus is gone, he thought, and imagined the world under shadow, a world that matched his loneliness; a world where stale air and barren land thrived, where fissures and cracks split the dust, sulfurous steam rising from their depths, choking the remaining life.

That world felt right. But it wasn't right. It was only inevitable. What could Cyprian do to stop the change? Poor, lonely Cyprian from the Taenaran forest, who could barely run or play, and had no friends. Or parents. It was hopeless, and he began to cry.

Why cry? a voice whispered. Cyprian looked up and around, searching through blurry vision for the light, the owner of the voice, a woodland nymph. There was naught by the earth, though Cyprian could feel the nymph's presence.

"I can't do it," he answered. "It's hopeless."

Nothing is hopeless, came the reply. *It is often difficult to see beyond despair. Yet hope is still there, if only you would look.*

"But what can I do against such terrible events?"

Much, she answered. The nymph, the light appeared from behind a small rock. She fluttered over to Cyprian and landed on his nose. Warmth and serenity overcame Cyprian as the soft glow filled his thoughts. *Anything you want if need is great enough.*

"I'm too small, too afraid to even start."

You have already started, my child. Size does not determine courage. Courage comes from the will to do what's right. And helps one continue to do what's right. Even when consequences are grim.

"I can't do this without Perseus," Cyprian said quietly.

That may be true, the nymph said. *This task may be beyond anyone's reach. But who can know until they've tried. You, Cyprian, you have become the owner of this task and the seeker of the book. You know this world's beauty, and understand what it will become if all is not set right. Would you let the world change so because of the uncertainty in your heart, uncertainty caused by sorrow?"*

"I wish it were not so," Cyprian said. "But how am I to forget the uncertainty, forget my sorrow?"

You do not have to forget your sorrow. But be at peace with it. For sorrow will come and go, as will happiness. When you do not fight your emotions, but embrace their pain and joy, only then will uncertainty give way to hope. And hope will see you through the most difficult of times.

I must go now, the nymph said and floated above Cyprian's head.

The light gently fluttered away, disappearing into the far woods, leaving Cyprian at peace, calm. He still felt sorrow from the loss of Perseus, but it did not rule him. It was a only a part of him. And Cyprian knew what he had to do, what he had to try to do. The book was his quest. Not for his sake. But for that of the world. And for Perseus.

Cyprian began walking. The road rose and fell as many fields and stretches of trees came on his right. He could feel the book north of the road he was traveling, but had he passed it already? Did he have far to go yet?

At each rise, Cyprian stopped and looked for the hill that Perseus had pointed out from the tower. Yet at each view there were multiple hills in the distance that looked the same. Hidden behind them were surely more hills. Which hill, if any, was the correct one? It was impossible to tell. And so Cyprian walked along the road until hunger reasoned him to stop.

He sat down on a crest in the landscape next to two fields, where he could see the woods beyond. Although it was not raining, dampness hung in the air. Cyprian set the pack before him and wrapped the cloak around his body. He opened the pack and sunk his hands in to grab an apple.

As he pulled the fruit from the pack a small ivory crucifix slipped from the interior and landed in the mud. Cyprian picked up the trinket, and was about to place it back in the bag when he noticed that no mud clung to the small figurine. As he turned the cross around, inspecting the flawless detail of the man, he felt a slight resistance, as if the piece did not wish to turn.

He placed the figure in the palm of his flat hand, in the direction in which he felt the most resistance. The figure slowly but immediately spun around on an invisible axis that would have been in the figure's chest; the head now faced northeast. The carving was a compass.

His appetite was all but gone, yet he ate a few bites of bland apple anyway. He trembled as it dawned on him what he was about to do. In a foreign land, alone, he was about to track down the most powerful artifact of the old world, which was trapped in the house of a *drakamor*.

Nausea welled up quickly, almost too quickly, as apple chunks filled Cyprian's throat. He barely turned his head away from the pack when whole bits of white flesh rained onto the ground. He couldn't do it; he couldn't be the one destined to get the book. Not alone. Despite what the nymph had said, he *was* too small, too weak. And his leg. He was a gimp, a cripple, a lame-foot, and a million other things he had been called in his life. This was a quest for the fate of the world, and he was being pulled into it, pulled into something that he couldn't do.

…the will of the Fates, the wind whispered. To Cyprian it sounded like Perseus.

"Was it the will of the Fates that you're dead?" Cyprian yelled back.

The wind swirled gently, coolly, but made no reply. It was in the silence, the stillness that Cyprian understood; it *was* the will of the Fates. They brought life as evenly as they brought death. Believing in the Fates meant accepting whatever came, good or bad, and then moving on. Perseus was gone, leaving Cyprian to complete the quest. It was how things were, and it was how things were meant to be.

Scared, nervous, and dreading what was to come, Cyprian unhurriedly cut the bottom portion off of the cloak so it would fit him appropriately, and stored the extra cloth in the pack. Then he sat, scared, wishing he didn't have to go on. Eventually, cold air found the weakness in the cloak's fibers, and Cyprian shouldered the bag and started off through the field, the crucifix as his guide.

He traveled through the field to the edge of the a forested hillock. Daylight was cast behind clouds, but looked even in the sky, on the edge of waning. The forest, however, was dark and frightful. Regardless, Cyprian entered, reminding himself that the shadows were nothing but shadows.

The brambles and brush were thick, often rising above Cyprian's head causing him to travel out of his way to get through and around. Many times, he became caught in a vine like the one alongside the river. The first time it happened, Cyprian panicked, struggled to get away, only succeeding in having the vine wrap tighter around his leg. When he calmed down and cut himself free, dark sap spilled from the vine's flesh, staining the earth. After that, Cyprian kept the knife free, and the vines were no more than a brief nuisance.

Familiar with traveling through woods, he walked quietly over the terrain. Yet there was a lot of noise, crashing in the brush behind him, too much, animals darting away from something unnatural to the forest.

Whenever the crashing started Cyprian's heart leapt into his throat. To keep from being trampled, he found the nearest tree and clung to it until the bounding animals passed. The animals sounded bigger than any woodland animal in the

Taenaran forest. Cyprian wondered what animals they were—something from this world? Some horrible hybrid of both?—though he did not wish to see them. So while he clung to the trees, he closed his eyes, fearing also to see what the animals were fleeing from.

The sixth or seventh time this happened, Cyprian had just crested the hillock. Four huge animals took off from somewhere distant and bounded through the dense thicket. They fled in his direction, and Cyprian hurried to a tree. One of the animals came so close that the air stirred on Cyprian's cheek. Sweat beaded on his forehead. He strained to breathe quietly. Three of the crashes continued forward, and Cyprian opened his eyes. Where was the fourth?

Three white tails were bounding away. Behind him, the last animal thrashed amidst the underbrush; the noise came from a lone spot. The animal was caught. Cyprian didn't have to look to know it was another white-tailed creature.

Heart thudding, breath heavy, he released the tree, wishing to be away from the captured animal as quickly as possible. Before Cyprian could move, a hushed note hit his ears, cutting through the animal's cries. Slowly, unnoticed, vines near the tree crawled along the ground toward him. The first vine reached his leg and wound around his ankle, continued winding. The song got louder.

He looked back in terror, searching the forest for the animal or owner of the song. He saw nothing; the forest was too dense with undergrowth. A second vine snagged his other leg. He cut free of it just as another reached his leg.

The song grew; the forest darkened; as Cyprian slashed through the vines, thick sap gushed from them like water from a pipe, spraying the earth. The song evened out, then dipped down an octave. There were no words where words should have been, but the intent of the melody was clear—sweet, gluttonous, and foul.

The animal let out one last bray through a fit of cracking branches and crunching leaves, and then fell silent with the song. The vines stopped advancing, but remained taut on Cyprian's legs. He cut through the last two vines and did not linger to remove their tendrils. He dashed forward, leaping over branches, cutting away thick brambles, and giving quick looks behind. Though he could not hear the song through his loud movements, the vines he had just passed moved, following him.

The brambles and trees grew sparse, replaced by intermittent trees and high brown grass, taller than Cyprian. Down the hill, between the trees, and through the grass he blindly flew, feeling the song, feeling vines glancing off his hooves. Ahead was a break in the trees, filled by sparse fog. A short burst of rain shot from the sky. The ground slickened. Cyprian ran like the wind, unconscious of his twisted foot.

Suddenly the ground dropped away, and Cyprian fell into the fog. He landed on hard ground and skidded; his breath was gone. He gasped, desperately searching for air, when rumbling and a loud honk caused him to look up.

He was on a wide muddy road between two short embankments. Two lights bore down on him faster than he thought possible. Cyprian rolled away from the lights, toward the far embankment. The lights, attached to a greenish bus, passed without slowing.

He regained his breath in a ditch opposite the forest he had been running through. His right knee throbbed with fiery pain. His head ached near the right temple, and when Cyprian touched it, there was wetness. He sat up; spots entered his vision, and then left, bringing everything into clear focus.

In the forest he had just come from the trees were swaying lightly but not of their own volition. Hundreds of brown vines wrapped throughout the high branches and twining down the trunks writhed like serpents, causing the trees to sway. The vines were seeking that which had just escaped.

It's the song, Cyprian thought, though he could not hear it. *A blood song.*

Cyprian knew he should be gone from this place. But anywhere could be just as dangerous. He was tired and his head ached, became heavy, forced him to lie back in the ditch.

Above the dry grass, through the fog, appeared white hair followed by an old face fraught with menacing wrinkles. The eyes of the face were crystal blue. The old man's mouth moved rhythmically, singing; yet Cyprian heard no song. The vines writhed in time with the mouth, coiling and twisting in lovely movements.

The old man's eyes locked on Cyprian, and then he smiled—a smile that would have been kindly had there not been blood, fresh and red, staining the yellow teeth. The smile dropped from the gruesome face, and the old man looked pensively at Cyprian. He paced along the hillock's edge, but came no closer. And, after a long minute, the old man lost interest, turned, and walked back into the forest.

Relieved, but wary Cyprian sighed. He ignored his soreness for the moment, took off his pack, slowly stood, and located the crucifix that had slipped from his hands when he fell. It lay in the road's middle, and when Cyprian picked it up it did not lay flat on his hand. The head pointed not only at the wooded hill he had been walking toward all day, but up it. He was here. He had made it.

"The will of the fates," he whispered to himself. Although hearing his own voice helped a little, Cyprian held no control over his bladder. Warmth ran down his leg as he looked up the mountain. "Tomorrow," he told himself. He would wait until morning.

As he walked back to his pack he noticed a side road a couple dozen yards down the road. In the morning he would follow that road as far as he could. Somewhere alongside that road was the destined house.

Cyprian found the excess cloak material in the pack and laid it in the bottom of the well-drained ditch. He lay on top, covered himself with the cloak, and used the pack as a pillow. Within minutes he was warm and as close to comfortable as was possible. He gave little thought to moving elsewhere.

Darkness soon crept over his little sleeping nest, and Cyprian fell into the disturbed slumber of the Ephialtes. Twice throughout the night small buses passed, startling him. He cringed in fear until realizing where he was and what the noises were. But the busses were not what disturbed his rest; he was so weary and battered that he quickly fell asleep after each had passed. It was his dreams that were disturbing.

Dreams of his parents leaving him, the details in the dream as real as life. The Taenaran River babbling softly, the sun shining through the fir trees, Cyprian warm and contented as he woke.

Dreams of Perseus, more dead than alive. But alive he was, lying alongside a tame river, drenched, sand and pebbles encrusting his face. A small stream of blood slipping from the corner of his eye. A small spider crawling next to his body, passing a hand that was clutching a curved horn; the surface of the object swirling with fallen moonlight.

Dreams of conquest. A sea filled with ships, sails spread full and menacing; whether it was one fleet or many was unclear, though they were all allied enemies. Dreams of battle, of massive armies meeting on a great plain. All the armies forged from legend, creatures that had not walked the earth for eons. It was a battle that would define the changing age.

Dreams that Cyprian wouldn't remember. Dreams that were not dreams, but visions from the ancient book. The relic was crying out from its captive perch, willing Cyprian to come. And Cyprian's mind was feeding off the call, seeing events in the book as they had happened, were happening, and would happen.

*   *   *   *

The road was filled with thick mats of fog when Cyprian awoke in the gray dawn. His head was stuffy and his nose was running—hardly the way to begin a day such as this. Perseus's cloak was loose around him, allowing cold air to invaded his nest. He pulled the cloak tighter, hoping that would fend off the cold. He wanted to return to slumber until the fog was gone and he was no longer groggy.

A thin puddle had welled up in the drain overnight. It was cold, and Cyprian felt its chill now that he was awake. It brought to mind warm baths, which Cyprian had never had. But now, the idea of one sounded like what he needed. A warm bath would lift his spirits, or the warmth of dreamless slumber. But that was not to happen.

Too miserable to fall back asleep, Cyprian sat up. The puddle of water beneath him sloshed. Keeping the cloak tight, he looked down the dreary road for any sign of Perseus, hoping that somehow he would be there, knowing he wouldn't. The road was empty. Cyprian pulled two apples from the pack and nibbled their tasteless, mealy flesh, staving off the errand for a couple of minutes, in which he hoped his courage would hold.

When the apples were gone Cyprian groggily stood. The air stole what little warmth he had, causing him to shiver as he packed away the soggy blanket, strapped the pack shut, and loaded it on his back underneath the cloak. Fearing to go yet not wanting to tarry, Cyprian took one difficult step after another, the knife and crucifix held in hands that were red, numb, and tingling, He soon came to the muddy road that led up the large hill.

The road rose over a short hump and then dipped a slight amount before beginning its ascent. Trees lined either side, but were only shadows through the fog. Cyprian sneezed. Quickly his body warmed. His fingers regained their feeling, and he felt the knife's handle between his fingers. He tightened his grip, compensating for the loose grip of the crucifix in his other hand.

Occasionally drops of water fell from the trees and landed amidst the forest leaves, the only sound. Cyprian sought the haze-filled forest for signs of danger in whatever form it might come. Yet there was nothing but the steady *drip drip* and the persistent fog; this was somehow worse than real danger.

He often glanced at the carving as he walked. And slowly, the head moved, turning to the left. The fog lifted from the road, though it remained thick in the forest, coming to the boundary of the trees, as if held captive by the forest. Cyprian took little notice. The carving's head swung, and he increasingly glanced at it, his stomach knotting with each step.

When the carving was pointing straight into the woods, Cyprian saw something in his peripheral vision. His heart stopped along with his feet, and he stood on quavering legs. A disruption, an anomaly in a small area of the forest was visible. The incongruence begged attention. Knowing he could not ignore it, Cyprian looked. But the forest looked normal. Trees and brambles blanketed by fog.

When Cyprian turned his head away, the disruption returned, was impossible to miss, and Cyprian looked at it as he focused on the road ahead. The anomaly was no more than a small area of trees half as wide as the road. But the trees were a darker shade than the rest. Cyprian kept his eye on one of the trees in the middle of the small group and turned his head toward the forest. Again, the disruption went away. But Cyprian walked to the tree he was looking at and reached out to touch it with the hand holding the carving.

His fingers went through the elm without resistance. Only, a shudder came over his mind, as if touched by an unexpected wind. Startled, he dropped the carving and pulled his fingers away. The carving landed at the tree's base, which seemed to shy away from the crucifix, as did the fog.

Cyprian marveled at the trees and studied those to either side of the middle elm. They were all elms, bark deeply furrowed and scaly, light gray, healthy. They were mere feet apart, yet they branched out quite low for the denseness of the forest. It was odd for an elm to say the least.

The fog around the carving lightened, and Cyprian searched through the haze into the forest depths. The trees were all hardwoods and evenly spaced. They branched out majestically, though they too seemed to shy away from the crucifix. The forest looked queerly cultivated, quite unlike the randomly scattered trees in every other natural forest.

Cyprian again put his hand up to the elm tree. It slid through with little more than a shudder. He kept his arm moving forward and walked, eyes closed. The shuddering surrounded his body, and Cyprian walked until it subsided, and then stopped, felt something crawling in his hair. With his hand, he brushed away a slimy mass. The small form popped beneath his fingers and flecks of black hit the ground. Cyprian wiped his neck and hands on his cloak.

The forest was entirely different past whatever boundary Cyprian had just come through. The fog was gone, though the sky was still overcast; the even, majestic trees were gone. In their stead was on an old path, dead trees lining either side. Black writhing slime infested the trees and the brambles at their base. The path wound slightly to the right and ended at a small clearing with a house.

Cyprian felt a light tickling sensation on his neck, and instinctively squirmed as he swatted another bit of the slime onto the ground. He turned to see that the elms he had come through were not there. Only a thin section of brush covered by a twisting mass of black worms lay at the foot of the path.

Another worm crawled onto Cyprian's neck. He spastically swatted it away before unclasping the cloak and throwing it to the ground. He slapped at his arms and neck and every other place he saw a worm until they were off him. A horrid screeching noise rose from the ground, and Cyprian turned, saw the worms swarming on his tattered cloak, eating it.

He gave a thought to the carving on the other side of the worm-covered brush. The worms on the cloak, now twice their original size left the tattered wool and slowly crawled toward Cyprian. The carving would have to be left behind, Cyprian decided, backing away from the worms; it had done its job.

Keeping to the middle of the path, he increased the distance between the worms and himself. Soon, they stopped their advance and crawled back to the entrance, allowing Cyprian to face forward and walk to the healthy clearing.

In the middle was a white house, dim and rotten, smelling of disease. Thick vines rose from the ground and climbed up the house's sides. The two windows on the front were broken, the door missing. From inside the house came laughter or an echo of laughter; Cyprian could not tell which.

He stood at the foot of the porch and stared at the blackness that was the doorway for an eternity, it seemed. The gray sky brightened. Behind him, as he focused, the soft, slick sounds of the black maggots squirming against one another became apparent. The noise was different than when they were feeding, but just as terrifying; it grew louder the longer he stood, attempting to push him forward, closer to the entrance. Yet the noise did not get closer, and the dark unknown was just as frightening. Cyprian remained still, summoning up courage to do what needed to be done.

Perseus came into his mind. His gentle manner, his knowledge, strength, humility. Cyprian wondered how he was supposed to defeat a *drakamor* without any of those qualities. It would be impossible. Almost impossible at least.

Thin beams of sun now shone through the thinning clouds. It warmed Cyprian to see, and gave him the last bit of courage he needed to take a step.

The first step was the hardest, but it was taken. And then the second, and a third. Cyprian walked up the porch stairs, onto the porch, stepping around boards that were broken or cracked. He crossed the small porch, not even noticing the latticework or flower that contrasted the rest of the house, and paused at the doorway, through which no light reached. Thinking of nothing more that Perseus, he stepped into cold dark lair of the *drakamor*.

*   *   *   *

Cyprian's dream the night before had indeed been true; that very night, Perseus lay unconscious alongside a creek after a long battle with the river demon. It was after he emerged from the water's depths and crawled up the shore that he finally fell under the spell of mortal and near fatal exhaustion. A lone spider crawled past Perseus as his lungs heaved heavily, trying to replace water with air, his chest rising and falling unnaturally in this charge.

It was well that Perseus knew nothing of his body, for he would have been repulsed by its feel; skin damp and wrinkled, sliced and poked, revealing raw flesh, irritated eyes with blood trickling from the corner, nose broken, and many more wounds from the river's wrath.

Perseus struggled between death and life on that shore, alone, yet not alone. For he had been carried downstream to a place that gave the river its name. The sand he had crawled onto was a narrow strip of marsh connected to a vast expansive marsh not a hundred yards downstream.

Beyond the narrow strip of marsh was a willow grove, and as Perseus dreamt deep dreams a woodland nymph called Diana, the same nymph who gave hope to Cyprian, found Perseus and set her stag to guard him while she bathed in her pool. The stag watched Perseus from beside the nearest tree until its mistress returned. Then, Diana mercifully took up the post as Perseus's life hung in the balance. She watched passively and untiringly until morning came and she knew he was still alive, pulling toward the light of day, not the light of death.

It was just after Cyprian entered the house that the nymph fluttered from her wooded perch to where Perseus lay, his breathing less harsh. She kissed his eyelids, soothing his eyes, cleansing debris from his wounds, bringing his pain into her body, seeing his life. Although there was ruthlessness and cunning in this man, there was also sadness, kindness, and tenderness. And love. The nymph took the form of a woman, one in Perseus's past, and kissed him deeply, breathing their life together, cleansing his lungs. Perseus's breath relaxed. He stirred, but did not waken.

The nymph returned to her tree, still in human form, and watched him in peace. She felt pity for him and his companion, and their quest; she left Perseus to his comfortable dreams; she guarded him from any danger while he slept on, hoping she had done enough to wake him in time. If he did not wake by nightfall, his companion would be lost.

AN OLDEN RYM[17]

As soon as Cyprian entered the house he was encased in heaving darkness. There was no light where there should have been from the open doorway. The doorway was gone, replaced by a lone speck of light in the far distance. Everything else was black and cavernous. Cyprian had not stepped into a house; he had stepped into a remnant of the old world.

He stepped backward, hoping to emerge onto the porch. His hoof clopped loudly on the wooden floor, and he remained shrouded in darkness. The clop hushed immediately. He felt the vastness of the lair, and knew he was trapped. Only now did he fully comprehend the foolishness of coming to such a place, and with only a knife as protection. In that first moment, he saw his death in this forlorn place and panicked, ran toward the small point of light. He ran until his breath raged and his lungs burned, no small feat for a satyr, yet the light never got closer.

The house heaved noticeably, and Cyprian felt its malicious oppression; then the house laughed—a muted laugh of delight and deviance.

Sensing the futility, sensing a change, Cyprian stopped running. The room had changed, the blackness constricted. Walls were on either side of him, a corridor. Cyprian put out his hand and felt the damp and spongy hardness of the decaying wall.

The plaster gave way and Cyprian's hand passed onto a soft, slick surface. He was oddly comforted though he knew he shouldn't be. The surface was warm and throbbing, like a womb to an unborn child. He pulled his hand away, and the soft surface was no more, had never been. It had been a trick of his mind. There was only the damp and spongy wall; it had been Cyprian's fingers that were warm and throbbing, no more.

He took three paces and felt a rough ridge running vertically along the wall. It was four inches wide and, beyond it, a slight breeze of cold, stale air replaced the plaster. Cyprian walked slowly, probing the clammy air for more wall, more ridge. After a tense moment he found another ridge a few feet ahead, and beyond that the wall returned. The opening was a doorway.

He passed more doorways as he walked along the corridor, oblivious of distance, oblivious of time. Only the dull pains of weary feet, then weary legs told him that either passed. At times the speck of light grew closer; at times it grew distant. The light, however, never changed in hue, and Cyprian realized it could not be the sun's light, which would wax and wane at the day's progression. Then, he doubted its existence at all. Perhaps the light too was a trick of his eyes. Or perhaps it was a trick of his mind, showing a speck of hope in this foul place. Or perhaps it was really there, and it was the darkness that was the trick.

Tiredness crept upon Cyprian, replacing fear and angst. The house had become comfortably warm, unlike last night's bed. And the many doors he passed were monotonous, always in the same pattern. Two steps to a doorway. Three steps to a doorway. Two steps to a doorway. The pattern repeated itself—two, three, two, two, three, two—and Cyprian grew weary, struggled to remain aware of his surroundings, aware of the impending danger. Even his fingers felt the fatigue of monotony, the knife in his hand no longer gripped firmly, but weakly.

After passing countless sets of doors, and seeing the speck of light grow and diminish countless times, Cyprian finally tired of the monotony. He leaned against the wall next to a doorway and let his body slide downward until he was sitting and resting his head on both hands. He was lost and the restless sleep of last night was a huge weight on his mind. If only Perseus was here; he would know where to find the strength to continue; he would know how to continue.

Just then, as Cyprian thought of Perseus, the house changed again. This change happened so discreetly that it was almost imperceptive. The air remained the same, but Cyprian knew it different, strange and evil. The silence remained; only it seemed to become louder. The darkness remained, yet it appeared to become darker.

Suddenly, the room behind Cyprian kindled with a soft yellow light. The source of the light remained still, and radiant beams shone into the hallway, lighting the corridor's far wall. Blinded, Cyprian shielded his eyes, then slowly peeked through his fingers. He focused on the shadows cast by his legs and allowed his eyes to adjust to the light.

The first view of the corridor showed that it stretched past the light's reach, and infinitely far as Cyprian could tell. Both sides of the hallway had doorways. Many evenly spaced doorways ran the length of the wall that Cyprian sat against. Two, three, two. The far wall had only one visible doorway though. It was down the hall a few paces, away from the light.

The walls were dingy; they had once been white, but were now covered with moldy splotches. In some spots the plaster had disintegrated and holes gave sight of thin wooden slats.

A footstep, heavy and hollow, sounded from the room with the light, startling Cyprian, paralyzing him. Then another, moving toward the door. The light moved too, nearing the doorframe.

Cyprian clutched the knife tightly, his only reassurance. As the footsteps and the light steadily came closer, a wave of dread swept through his body. He managed to find his feet and back away, but he could walk no faster than a crawl. His eyes remained fixed on the doorway.

With a small moment of knee-weakening terror, Cyprian bumped into the opposite wall. The plaster bent, gave way to the comforting softness beneath, the womb, thumping rhythmically, drawing Cyprian into its warmth. A candle, held by a hand, bloated and gray, fingernails warped with grotesque curves and gashes, emerged from the doorway and glided forward. The womb faded, hardened into the wall it had always been.

As Cyprian edged along the wall, his hand passed onto a doorframe, then grasped emptiness. The distended arm attached to the hand drifted through the doorway, followed by a shoulder. The body turned, and Cyprian saw long black locks of hair, familiar hair, as his shoulder blades passed over the doorframe. It was...

"Perseus," he said, as the figure walked through doorway, body full and discolored, nose horribly crushed, dark gray cuts across his face, body, and through his clothes; his hair was wet and matted to his forehead; water seeped down his chest; it was a Perseus dead and forgotten, except for his eyes. They were keen and intelligent.

"I'm here," the corpse murmured hoarsely, a black maggot crawling out of his nose.

Cyprian screamed, passed beyond the doorjamb, and fell into darkness, landing on his pack. The light was gone, clouded by a black fog, and Cyprian was as relieved as he was terrified. However, something wispy landed on his neck and crawled toward his hair, doubling his terror. Cyprian screamed and brushed away the black worm. The pack beneath him sunk toward the ground as if deflating. Cyprian loosened the straps, fearing what the pack now held. The high-pitched screeching of the worms filled the room, as if hundreds of fledgling birds were there, pecking each other in desperate starvation.

Cyprian left the pack and ran, slammed into a wall as hard as rock, smashing his forehead and nose. He landed hard on the wooden floor, and the knife flew from his hand, bounced off the wall, and skittered across the floor lost in the darkness.

Stars danced in his dark vision. And although he was lying on the ground, he was overcome with vertigo. The darkness spun, carried the cluster of stars into a spiral. Cyprian feared to close his eyes lest they stay that way, and endured his torture wide-eyed until the dizziness left and stars were gone, and the darkness returned to its placated self.

Head heavy with pain, Cyprian got on all fours and crawled along the wall, away from the maggots. Their screeching multiplied, amplified in the room as it should not have done, and Cyprian crawled faster. He soon reached a corner of the room and was forced right. After another couple seconds he felt a doorway along the wall. It could have been the same doorway he had entered, through which was the hallway and Perseus's corpse; but for all he knew it could also be a different one. Taking his chances, wishing to be away from the maggots, Cyprian hurriedly crawled through the doorway, felt nothing where there should have been floor, and fell downward. His hand landed a foot lower, on the top step of a set of stairs, and folded under itself, sprained. Unable to catch himself, Cyprian tumbled down the remaining stairs, which seemed to go on forever.

At last the descent stopped and Cyprian lay on a stone floor, uninjured save for small aches and the twinge in his left wrist. He struggled to his knees and right hand and painfully crawled forward, into the heavy silence of the room. He crawled across the gritty stone, hands and knees hitting small, elongated objects that clattered hollowly, until his arm nearly gave way. In silent, lost frustration he stopped and sat. The ancient book was a small thought in his mind. There was no way he could find it by himself—not in this darkness. And he was weary. Too weary to continue.

Thankfully, things were quiet. And as long as they remained that way, Cyprian would stay in this spot. It was the most comfort he had felt since the morning on Thaeron.

Without warning, the air began to stir, moving past Cyprian on all sides and building to a great speed. It was as if the room had filled with ghosts that flew about in a whirlwind of malice.

Cyprian would have cried if he had any tears left. As it was, he cringed and sank as low to the ground as he could. He prayed to Titania, the goddess of life, to Diana the goddess of nature, hoping that this strange, diseased place fell inside their realm.

Please, he mouthed, though his tongue was parched. *Help me from this evil place.*

As if in response, the air thickened to a soup, making the next words catch in Cyprian's throat. He found it impossible to speak; and from the darkness came laughter, sinister and happy.

*   *   *   *

Perseus felt life and breath, and he opened his eyes and knew he was alive. And for the moment he was safe from the world's harms. The river was no longer swollen and angry. The water's edge lapped gently, reverently at his feet. Chirruping permeated the forest softly. The sound was sweet—as sweet as the air that had warmed and blanketed Perseus since the morning. It was a morning in which peace had woven cozy thoughts over the harsh reality of broken bones, deep cuts, and water saturated lungs, turned that reality into a dream, from which Perseus was waking.

On this night of waking, an orange-red sunset blazed; it was a sunset worthy of the ancient kings and their queens. The sky cast brilliant colors on the trees, weaving gold with black into a color to be awed. Just beyond a thin stretch of green and purple marsh grass was a grove of weeping willows that were healthy and strong. The trunks split majestically into branches that swept up, outward, and then downward, clothing the grove's inside from prying eyes. The ground beneath the trees was slightly elevated above the marsh, the grass healthy and manicured, though not cut.

Perseus raised his head and spit sand from his mouth. The curved horn of the demon remained in his right hand, spoils of the battle, though Perseus did not remember keeping it. He carefully set the horn aside and struggled to his knees, using his sword as a crutch. Once on his feet, Perseus plunged the sword into the sandy soil and brushed away the grit that crusted his face, hair, and clothes. Grains of sand irritated his eyes, and Perseus went down to the water to wash it away.

The river, no longer a threat, was refreshing and nice, and Perseus stripped off his clothes and washed them clean of the sand.

"Very nice," a woman's voice said from behind.

Startled, Perseus almost fell. He gained his balance and wrapped his shirt around his waist before turning around.

A woman with long, dark brown hair stood at the edge of the marsh grass, a willow branch wrapped around her fair head. A fine bow, intricately carved with wild beasts, was clasped in one hand. A small buckskin was draped over her right shoulder, padding the quiver that rested on her back. Otherwise, the woman was naked, radiant in the failing light. Her lips held a slim smile, her eyes a calming spirit. Perseus gazed, unable to speak. She closely resembled Andromeda. Perseus wished it was Andromeda, at this moment longing for his wife more than anything. The woman's smile shifted, if indeed she was a woman, into a knowing smile.

"Forgive me," he said, his tongue loosened. "I thought I was alone."

"You are never alone," she said, gesturing at the woods. "There are always creatures to give you company whether you wish it or not."

The woman laughed. The sound mingled nicely with the running water and chirruping crickets. Her breasts swayed freely and Perseus's eyes were drawn to their beauty. A gleam came to the woman's eye.

"Distracted easily," she mused. A soft glow briefly flickered in her eyes, and Perseus knew that this was no mortal. "Yet that is to be forgiven."

"Thank you, my lady," Perseus said, "if I may call you that."

"You may."

"Is it to you that I owe my life?" he asked.

"A strong will is to what you owe your life," the nymph said. "I merely sped the healing."

"I am in your debt, then."

"Yes," the nymph said.

"Though I am bound to repay you, I beg your forgiveness. I must make haste toward the destination that I seek."

"Yet you linger by the pool, washing your clothes." She spoke softly, the smile remaining on her lips.

"I am still weak and wished for a brief stay of rest."

"So I see," she said, then paused. "If you knew of your companion's fate, perhaps you would not linger."

"Cyprian," Perseus whispered. "What of him?"

"He is strong and has survived much," the nymph began, her eyes glowing with sadness. "Though he has come upon that which he does not have strength for. The trees brought me word of the fallen bridge and your fight with the river. Though your fate was sealed under its wrathful waves when I arrived, I found Cyprian and knew him to be one of my children. I followed and spoke with him, relieving him from as much sadness as I dared—it would have done him no good to rid him of it completely. But I gave him the hope he needed to continue, and watched over him until he entered a forsaken woodland, where unnatural things abound. When I returned to my grove you were washed up on my shores, and I bent my will to protecting you till your life *or* death was certain. It was morning when I was sure you would live, and only then did I speed the healing of your wounds. By that time, Cyprian had entered the lair of the *drakamor*. He is alive but will not make it till the morrow."

The nymph fell quiet, and Perseus pondered her words. As he was, he could not make it to the hill and have enough energy left to fight.

"Do not fret," the nymph said as if in understanding. "You will bathe in my pool and drink of my drink. It will give you strength, perhaps enough, to save young Cyprian and to retrieve the book."

"You know of the book?" Perseus asked.

"I know much about you, Perseus," she said, and then more than ever she sounded and looked like Andromeda, smile curving up at the corners of her mouth, eyes gleaming with a love as deadly as it was kind. "Though there isn't enough time to speak of such things. Follow."

In a twirling mist, the woman vanished; a small fluttering light took her place. The sun was gone and the forest was dim, yet Perseus clearly saw where he was going. He felt at ease, his heart light. He knew Cyprian was in trouble, but he needed strength. And so he gathered his belongings and followed the nymph into the Willow Grove, focused on her immediate purpose.

Tis a powerful thing, the nymph spoke, as she led him swiftly. And Perseus knew she was speaking of the horn.

"Yes," Perseus said.

In time, it will serve you well.

"You have the gift of foresight, then."

The gift of sensibility, the nymph replied.

They passed through the sweeping willow branches and through the fragrant grass to a quiet pool carved into the ground. Its sides were a smooth, white rock rounded along the edges. The nymph landed on the side of the pool, and shone brighter than before, reflecting the pool's starlight.

Do not be shy, she whispered.

Perseus laid his clothes and sword by the water's edge, and lowered into the pool. The water was delightfully warm, and Perseus sunk below the surface, felt the last bit of weariness leave his body. When his head emerged, it stayed warm, shielded from the outside cold. He ran fingers through his hair, and found the river debris gone.

Drink, the nymph said.

Perseus cupped his hands and drank from the pool crisp, sweet nectar. Warmth washed through his body, over his thoughts. He sank deep into comfort, where visions came and went, of May Fair where the food was rich and filling, of his sister, of his parents, of Andromeda, of all that he loved and made him happy.

Abruptly the visions cut off, taking their words and pictures, but leaving their happiness. The forest returned to Perseus's vision, and he did not feel afraid; he felt purposeful.

I have spared you as much time as I would, the nymph said, stirring Perseus from his thoughts. *You must go now.*

Reluctantly, but with purpose, Perseus exited the pool and dressed. The nymph fluttered to a goatskin and a leather pouch that were hanging on a tree branch beside the pool.

Take this pouch for your prize, she said. *A gift fit for the gods, as is the goatskin. Your friend will need the draught if he is to live. I bid you farewell, Perseus, son of Telemachus, husband of Andromeda. My thoughts go with you.*

Perseus nodded, for a brief moment feeling the nymph's coy smile. He placed the horn in the pouch, buckled his sword round his waist, and slung the skin over his shoulder before bowing deeply. "Thanken yow, my lady," he spoke in olde tongue. "Ywis, I shal remember yow alderbeste."[18]

The nymph fluttered kindly as Perseus turned and ran out of the willows, into the woods, headed for Donaldson Hill.

Fear not the darkened wood, the nymph whispered. *My breath will protect you till the morrows moon. Yet be wary of the lair of the drakamor. It is evil, advanced beyond my grace...*

Perseus ran as swift as the wind. Yet it was on the wind that the nymph gave one last cry of wisdom....*but not beyond your childhood,* she said. And then her voice was gone, and Perseus was left alone with the darkness to guide him.

*   *   *   *

The air quickened. Then came pain, thin and sharp. It felt as if someone were lightly and repeatedly slashing Cyprian with a knife. He remained crouched on the ground, arms covering his face, fearing to cry out, fearing to move as the pain broadened, traveling along the entirety of exposed flesh. Air sought the insides of the shallow wounds, drew blood up and outward, and carried it into the air as a red mist. With searching, searing fingers, the wind crawled beneath Cyprian's body and lifted him. He fought to keep his face from harm as his stomach and other newly exposed flesh was cut, new blood drawn forth.

On the edge of unconsciousness, the whirring air died, the slashing receded. Cyprian dropped the few inches to the floor and lay quietly sobbing into his hands. Blood, cold and wet, ran from him in slow streams. He felt weak and dizzy, and gasped uncontrollably, the air difficult to breathe.

Tears ran into the wounds on his arms and stung. The cuts on his stomach gaped against the stone floor and soaked up the dirt. Cyprian curled into a ball and screamed as the cuts flexed, burning anew.

The house was still, and in that Cyprian felt a small amount of comfort. He took deep breaths, and slowly calmed down. The tears stopped. There was no light in this room, yet Cyprian could see it clearly in his mind. He was in a stone cellar, an old wooden staircase along the back wall. Underneath the staircase was a pile of broken wooden beams. Throughout the room strewn randomly on the dirty floor were skeletons, both animal and human. All of the skeletons were intact, fused together at the joints.

Strangest of all in the room were the two broken cellar windows, through which the moonlight shone, through which Cyprian could see the tops of the trees surrounding the clearing. The trees were cracked and fragile, lifeless, yet they swayed and rustled in light sweeping movements, speaking to him, telling a tale, showing a tale of Perseus running through the woods, a silver aura surrounding his body.

"Must you torment me?" he whispered hoarsely.

A drop of blood tickled his brow, and Cyprian wiped the sticky stream away with an equally sticky hand. Black spots lined with light grew in his vision. Chill swept through his bones. Sleep came to mind. He wanted to sleep.

Wearily, Cyprian fought off the thought, dreading what would happen if he were to fall asleep, though he was too tired to think of what that might be. He focused on the room, on the stairwell, and pushed to his hands and knees, wailing for the pain. He turned toward the stairwell with a great effort and crawled forward, collapsed.

His body hurt; the floor hurt, then became as comfortable as a pine bough bed lined with leaves. Cyprian's eyes drooped and closed, his breath evened. He heard the trees whispering from afar, then knew only his fading dreams.

*   *   *   *

Perseus heeded the nymph's words and gave no care to the surrounding woods and their perils. He ran hard, holding a course northwest. Through pastures and fields his path went. Over fences, through thorny thickets, and across the dirt road that Cyprian had followed one day prior. Perseus flew through the woods with great purpose, slicing through brambles with his sword as if they were no more than clouds.

He felt good and evil in the woods as he passed, a ghost to them all. Small, woodland creatures scuttled here and there. Bloodthirsty earth. A song was being sung. Perseus glanced to his left. Close enough to be seen in the moonlight, vines writhed in torment, choking the trees they infested, choking a small animal caught in their clutches. Perseus flew on, the nymph's last words returning to his thought.

...but not beyond your childhood, the nymph had said. And it made perfect sense. The childhood rhyme that was a warning in the olden days. A warning, passing down knowledge of the ancient spirits. Perseus silently thanked the nymph and pondered the last few lines of the riddle, musing at their hidden secrets, their knowing words.

The words went in and out of Perseus's mind, though he could make no sense of them. In this rhyme, the wisdom was riddle. One that Perseus hoped he could solve before arriving at the house.

At last he came to a second road, and the riddle fell second to his senses. This was a road he had expected. Though there was no sign, Perseus knew it as the Fairfield Road. He was at the base of Donaldson Hill, close to David's road, close to the book.

Perseus turned left on the muddy road, passing few houses, all long asleep in the waning night, except for one that had a strange, orange light in one of the windows. It read: *psychic.* Perseus passed by the house with hardly a thought, quickly forgetting the light blue siding and brown shutters. The light however remained in his thoughts. Until, that is, he came upon the road he was looking for.

Perseus relaxed his pace as he turned up the road. He had been running for over an hour through the thick entanglements of forest underbrush, yet his breathing was regular and his legs felt strong.

As he jogged he took note of everything in the surrounding woods. He was looking for something unusual, though he did not know what. Even this close, even though he could almost smell the *drakamor's* evil, it would be difficult to find the house. The old parchments spoke that a *drakamor* could be nearly invisible if he wished not to be found. And this *drakamor* held the book of Antioch.

Perseus searched the hardwood forest thoroughly for any disruption. There were maple, elm, and ash scattered loosely about, moonlight and starlight shining through their crooked boughs. Few noises were to be heard, and Perseus gave the few he did hear no thought; they were only branches or leaves falling to the ground.

Halfway up the mountain, he found the disruption he was looking for. On his left the forest grew sparse and evenly spaced. Even before Perseus could look for any other sign of queerness, he saw a silvery glittering on the side of the road. He neared the object and slowed to a walk, noticed the elms in front of him were translucent in the light of the moon, their bottoms distorted by the glitter.

It appeared that the elms were there, yet Perseus knew they were not. There were also brambles between the trees, stiff and dead, and at the same time there were none; the middle of the translucent brambles was flattened. Something or someone had recently passed through them. *Cyprian.* He had passed through the brambles had also passed through hoards of squirming black maggots that were there, and at the same time were not.

The silvery object, Perseus saw, was the crucifix. It laid half in the translucent elms and half out. Perseus reached down, put his hand through the elm without resistance, and picked up the carving. It calmed him from the dread that had not yet reached consciousness. He held the ivory man through the elm trees. From its silvery light he saw half of his cloak lying on the ground beyond the brambles.

Perseus drew his sword and walked through the translucent trees, on the path that was worn through the brush. Small snags of brush, real brush, caught on his clothes, and in the dim light, translucent maggots caught hold of Perseus's shirt and appeared to chew through it. But the shirt remained whole. Perseus brushed the ghostly maggots from his clothes and walked down the path.

Dead, gangly trees stood still like menacing statues, casting ominous shadows in their wake. On their branches were more translucent maggots that huddled and writhed in masses, which drooped from the limbs. On a whisper of wind came an inaudible screeching sound that Perseus ignored. Then, as he advanced and saw the house, came laughter.

A thing of evil it was, the laughter and the house. And like most evil, it hid behind veils of goodness—tricks of the mind and heart. Surrounding the house was death and barren woodland, stripped of life long ago, forsaken. The house itself appeared to be no more than a simple country house from this world. It was one story, a porch and a chimney left to rot with the ages.

And then Perseus's eyes caught on the untouched lattice at the side and lingered there, searching the craftsmanship for flaw it did not hold, finding the rose, white and perfect, clinging to a green vine. It was innocence in the midst of despair, benevolence in the midst of malevolence, life in the midst of death, and it clung to a shred of the rhyme that had been running through Perseus's head, became forgotten as a shriek filled the house. Cyprian's shriek.

Perseus ran up the stairs, onto the porch, and into the gloom, sword and cross held in front of him. He stopped once inside, surprised by the stale, oppressive air.

The entryway of the small house was lit with harsh moonlight that shone through the doorway. Three exits led out of the entryway—one to either side of Perseus, and one at his front. The two on the sides were doublewide doorways without doors. Each was rimmed with broken molding, and each led into small rooms. In front of Perseus was a framed exit that led down a darkened corridor.

Though Perseus could see the entryway and doors clearly, they seemed an apparition. All were translucent and overlaying a separate room of unmeasured vastness. This room no light penetrated. It was blacker than night, and this was where the oppression came from.

Cyprian screamed again, and the sound pierced Perseus's ears with pained sadness. It echoed throughout the house, the entryway, and the black room, though which direction it came from was difficult to tell. The scream's echo multiplied and shifted, then slowly faded. It was in the hallway in front of Perseus that the echo died last. And that way, Perseus took.

The empty vastness flew by him as if in fast forward as he ran down the short hallway to another room. Again he stopped and the reeling blackness came to a halt. Perseus was in another vast room of blackness, which overlaid a smaller room with an old fireplace and a broken table. Three windows let in a strange light that was filtered through the oppression. On the floor were the broken, splintering legs of an old wooden chair. Next to them were Cyprian's pack and knife.

Beside the corridor's entryway was another doorway. An old door hung ajar on the bottom hinge. Small, frantic grunts came from the darkness beyond. Perseus wished to yell, to tell Cyprian he was coming. But he refrained. Surprise might be the only chance he had to kill the *drakamor*. Or to save Cyprian's life.

As Perseus picked up the knife, the lattice from the porch crept into his mind and spread. The image burned and itched as the answer to the riddle. It was the answer, somehow, but Perseus couldn't think straight, couldn't see beyond the house's oppression and Cyprian's tortured grunts.

He tucked the knife behind his belt and drew his sword before stepping through the door. He walked quickly and quietly down the short flight of stairs and found a stone-lined room, translucent beneath the house's darkness. Yet down here, the darkness seemed to brood, as if this was its center.

Cyprian knelt in the middle of the dirty, bone-littered floor, arms raised covering his face. Two small windows graced the room with moonlight, showing the many cuts on Cyprian's body, and the blood that seeped from them. There was more blood on Cyprian than Perseus had seen any man lose and keep his life.

Hovering above Cyprian was the *drakamor*, though only its eyes and a small sliver of skin were visible in the direct moonlight. The skin was pale, taught over a lean midsection. The eyes glowed a fierce golden haze, and looked up from their labor, seemingly startled.

Perseus brought his sword over his head and threw it in a rage, directly between the creature's eyes. The sword hit its mark, but passed through the *drakamor* as if the creature were made of air. The eyes changed, and the *drakamor* laughed; the house laughed with it, heaving and spewing.

Perseus was already advancing toward the *drakamor*, the crucifix held in front of him. The creature stopped laughing; it withdrew from delight into calculation—but not fear as Perseus had hoped. Then the eyes and body disappeared into the darkness. The air began twirling.

Old nails and bits of loose stone swirled in a tempest. The moonlight clouded over as if a black fog had settled. Cyprian cried out weakly as Perseus swept him up and covered the small, feverish body with his own.

Bending his mind to the cross, Perseus pushed the swell of darkness away; faint moonlight returned to the room, enough for Perseus to see the cellar's silhouette. He located the stairwell and ran up it as the whirlwind shrieked. Bits of debris pelted his back and head. Two nails stuck into his skin, yet Perseus ran on. The *drakamor* howled with laughter and picked up Perseus's sword.

"Perseus," Cyprian whispered, his dark and swollen eyes opening a sliver. Perseus hugged Cyprian tightly, but dared not answer.

The tempest followed them into the small hallway. There was light at the end, but it clouded over and everything was cast into shadow. Perseus heard a familiar ring; soft pings of debris were hitting his sword, getting close. The *drakamor* was gaining.

The blackness grew darker, almost extinguished the small corridor of the one story house. Perseus focused on the crucifix, on the hallway he was in, and the blackness leveled. The house groaned in delightful rage. The air thickened and the house sank deeper into darkness. The corridor lengthened.

"Perseus," Cyprian said again. Perseus could barely hear him above the howling wind. "I tried...ied to find the book." Cyprian coughed up blood. "But I...couldn't do it."

The satyr shuddered and coughed again onto Perseus's shoulder. When the fit passed, he continued speaking, calmly, his voice stronger. And Perseus could hear every word as if they were being spoken inside his head.

"The trees were whispering...speaking...could see it, the strangeness, sadness...they..." Cyprian coughed again; flecks of redness ran down his chin. "...sang." The young voice paused before continuing, speaking weakly, softly, sweetly. "...lyf divine, softe and smal, the weed grewen...it shynes, tere the vertue fro the deedly temple whyte..."

Cyprian's words, the words of the rhyme, echoed in Perseus's head. In ear shattering booms, visions of the fireplace in the main room of his father's palace in Thessaly streamed into remembrance. His father was telling the ancient rhyme as he often did at Perseus's request. And although Perseus had not seen it then, behind his father had been a vase of flowers, as there were often flowers kept around the house for his mother.

In truth, there may not have been flowers then, but this was as Perseus saw it now, as the *drakamor's* lair splintered beneath him, furious, devilish, maliciously amused. And as the *drakamor* closed the distance to Perseus, it was his father's deep and loving voice that rang in his ears in the long ago comfort of home. And the vase of flowers that were purple. And the childhood rhyme that had kindled in Perseus a flame. And the flowers and the rhyme and the one line stuck out of the rhyme that was a riddle, an old childhood riddle—*cleave the life from death itself,* the way his father had told it. *Tere the virtue fro the deedly temple whyte,* the way the old book told it.

In his memory, the flowers and his father's voice, and the flowers turned white and shimmering, silvery with morning dews against the palace wall that melted into darkness and the flowers became one, the vase spinning round with green swirls until it was a vine sunken in the earth, clinging to a lattice that was perfect with grace and beauty and was life in a place of death.

And Perseus knew as the vision faded and the tempest returned, and the soft pings of debris against his sword became reality once more and were close, raised above his head, that it was the flower outside the house that was the *drakamor's* heart. That was the life that needed torn.

The sword blade swung downward. Perseus dove to the side of the hallway, cradling Cyprian. Cold steel grazed his thigh; the razor sharp blade stuck in the ground. Perseus kept the flower in his mind and focused on the cross. The blackness diminished, allowing Perseus to jump to his feet.

The house groaned, the floorboards opened up, and the sword came free in a jerk. It moved backwards with an invisible force and then moved forward. In that instant, the black chasm lightened and Perseus saw the end of the hallway. He leapt out of the corridor, into the entryway when, once again, the blackness bent, distorting the entryway into an endless room.

The front door was visible, but it stood still as Perseus ran toward it. Then it came closer by a step, but no more. The soft pings of debris on sword again gained ground. Sweat poured from Perseus's brow. It was difficult to run.

As the pings gained and were just behind Perseus, the crucifix heated slightly, speaking its own language, and Perseus understood. He whirled mid-stride and threw the crucifix, aiming for the blankness beneath the raised sword. Dirt and stone pelted the crucifix in a swarm of anger, yet the carving hit its mark. Flames leapt from the ivory whiteness as it clung to the air beneath the sword. The house let out a high shriek and the blackness faded, leaving only the entryway of the decaying house, through which was the first tinges of dawn.

Surrounding the house were maggots, black as death, a huge squirming sea that covered the trees, ground, and porch. Perseus lunged for the door. The blackness behind him strengthened, nearly pulled him and Cyprian backward into the gloom. But Perseus heard the deafening shrieks of the maggots and felt the cool morning air, and knew he had made it. His feet landed in the maggots on the porch. He nearly lost his footing, and dropped to a knee to keep from toppling over.

The maggots immediately gnawed through his boots and pants, increasing in size. They crawled onto his skin and gnawed at his flesh. Ignoring the pain, Perseus turned for the white rose. He loosened the knife from his belt and dodged his sword as it sliced through the front wall, leaving a black mist where it had cut.

At the latticework Perseus's eyes caught on the flower, and he stopped for a moment, staring, transfixed by the rose's beautiful petals, shimmering in the first light. He was unable to move, unable to think, and barely felt the blade of the sword slice into his calf, deep into his flesh, or the maggots crawling into his boots and up his legs, disintegrating his pants as they went, ingesting his skin. Some maggots found new flesh at his thigh and others were crawling higher.

But it was only the rose that he saw. It was singing to him a beautiful melody of life. The rose itself was life, and nothing else seemed to matter.

Cyprian heard the song too, though he heard it through his mutilated body. The song tapped into his wounds, drawing out more blood, converging on his last life. Weakly, desperately, Cyprian cried out to Perseus.

The rose's song faltered against Cyprian's. Perseus felt Cyprian's pain, knew it was because of the flower. The rose was pretending to be life, and Perseus saw it for the evil it was. The rose petals seethed behind their master; they held tiny veins that throbbed with greedy desire, and were filled with the blood of their pray—Cyprian's blood. The petal's silvery hue was the morning light held captive; the green stalk was riddled with lust and envy, and was rippled with tiny poisonous thorns, which guaranteed slow death to anyone who touched them.

This rose was the bane of life, and with a long sweep Perseus sheared the flower from its stalk.

Morning light spilled from the stalk and flower, and as the rose fell toward the ground, a deep roar betook the house; the blackness shuddered and thrashed, the walls heaved outward, threatened to topple. The maggots melted together, fell to the floor, through the floor, and disintegrated; those on the ground slipped into the barren earth without a trace.

The roar continued.

The morning light returned to the sky and the stalk gushed black blood where Perseus had sliced through it. The flower gushed the same as it finally hit the dry earth below. The latticework decayed; at once it slumped and fell.

The roar morphed into a low deep rumble, shaking the entire house violently, and then stillness came, though the roar echoed throughout the forest, sending waves of dank breath across the land.

After the blood stopped gushing, the vine wilted and clung to the broken lattice as nothing more than a weed. The flower blackened and disintegrated into dust, and lay as a small pile in the calm twilight.

Perseus reaffirmed his hold on a cold and limp Cyprian, replaced the knife into his belt, and looked to the house. His sword was stuck through the wall above where his head had been when he cut the flower. Perseus stepped underneath the blade; it was less than an inch from his scalp.

He said a quiet prayer and walked to the porch stairs, passing three other gashes in the wall, which gaped open as if the house had been flesh. He sat down and opened his shirt. Perseus laid the satyr next to his warm chest and poured a trace of the nymph's draught into his mouth. Cyprian did not swallow.

BIGINNE AL NEWE[19]

All was quiet in the forest, and Perseus felt the surroundings peering over his shoulder as if they knew what was to come. Minutes passed as slowly as years, and still Cyprian did not swallow. But neither did the liquid escape, and Perseus clung to that fiber of knowledge. He placed his ear over Cyprians mouth, but felt and heard no breaths. However, Cyprian's chest did rise and fall slightly, almost too slight to see. And there was a faint heartbeat in the small chest, though too faint for Perseus's liking.

He gave Cyprian another dose of the water and watched. Water dribbled from the satyr's mouth and ran down his cheeks in slow streams. Yet, not all of the water spilled. Inside Cyprian's mouth was a shallow pool, which slowly drained into his throat. When Perseus took Cyprian's pulse again, he thought it felt stronger.

When the pool was gone, Perseus once again poured the water into Cyprian's mouth. For the first time, a full hour after the first draught, Cyprian's lips moved lightly, closed of their own will. The satyr swallowed painfully, and Perseus gave him another dose.

By the time the sun crested the quiet ring of trees, Cyprian's heart was pumping strong enough for his wounds to resume bleeding. Perseus retrieved the half cloak from near the roadway, and laid the unconscious Cyprian on it in at the base of the porch. His mutilated body was pale, the color draining through the gashes.

Perseus uncapped the goatskin once more and tipped it to Cyprian's parched and bloody lips. He could not tell if the liquid had been swallowed or if it remained on the pallet so he poured more.

Cyprian unexpectedly coughed, sending a mixture of blood and water into Perseus's face. Yet Perseus saw the satyr swallow, and knew that precious water had gone down. He put a sixth dose in Cyprian's mouth and kissed him lightly on the forehead.

"I shan't be gone long," he said.

Leaving the sun as guard he limped into the house, the wound in his calf gaping open. He passed by the two wide doors on either side of the entryway, knowing the ancient book was in one of them, and walked down the hallway to the kitchen. He grabbed the pack and returned to the sunlight.

Using a small amount of nectar and the remaining elderberries, Perseus made a salve, which he gently applied to Cyprian's body. Almost immediately the bleeding evened, and Cyprian moaned. Perseus gave him another swig of water, which was swallowed thirstily and without difficulty.

Then, and only then did Perseus spare two drops of the nectar for the gash in his own leg. After which, Perseus removed the nails that were stuck in his back and rested in the sun, keeping watch over Cyprian, giving him small sips from the goatskin at regular intervals.

At noon, when the sun was at its highest and Cyprian was as peaceful as possible, Perseus chanced a longer look inside the house. He walked first into the room on the right, where his sword was stuck in the wall. Above the gash, the wall was stained black, as if fire had ravaged that lone spot.

With great effort, Perseus removed his sword from the wall and inspected its blade. It was good steel and the blade held true. The hilt, however, was different, as if it had been partially dissolved where clasped by the *drakamor*. Perseus stuck the sword into its scabbard, exited the room, and walked across the entryway.

He lingered at the doorway, inhaling the scent of the room, flowers, dim and dingy in the aged musk of the house. In one corner were two small skeletons that were clean and well preserved, fused together as if they had been holding each other. Clasped in one of the skeleton's hands was a small crystalline bottle, the cap off.

Clothes and other cloth lay in tatters around the bones. Sprite cans, crushed and disfigured, small, clear wrappers, hundreds of tiny sticks with red and blue tips, along with many other trinkets were also scattered about. On the wall above David and Billy's remains a rectangular piece of cardboard was tacked into the plaster and read: *Star Crunch.*

Perseus looked at the scene without emotion. It was the only way he knew to face such events and be able to continue. As he glanced around the room, he noticed a bulge on the floor that blended in with the dirty brown wood. Yet as Perseus walked toward the bulge, he saw that it was black and not brown, and it stood out brilliantly against the wooden grains.

It was a book—the book. The book lay face down and open, its brilliant black cover outshined only by the intricate golden lettering on its face—ancient lettering that few knew. Though Perseus had not known what it read in the vision, he could read it now.

"Golden aventure,"[20] he whispered. The book of Antioch was a book of golden chance in this world.

The book called to Perseus, and he longed to look inside its pages. Although he had seen the pages in the vision, he sensed that their effect would be different now, all consuming. He had the fate of two worlds in his grasp.

Perseus scooped the book into his arms, closing it as he did so. He was the warder of the book, and wished to play his part and be done with it. He would not look inside unless…

…*unless I must*, he thought reluctantly and gravely.

*   *   *   *

The book was both light and heavy, and shimmered as Perseus took it out into the sunlight. He knelt with his back to Cyprian, and carefully bound the book in a swatch of cloak. As he did so Cyprian's eyes opened suddenly, though they were glassy and white.

"The bible is sauf," Cyprian said, his voice dull and even. Perseus turned and gasped at sight of the satyr's eyes. "Though it is variaunt, disordinaunt, and eek straunge. Previdence has vanished; the clooth is blank. Unwist is all that is certein."[21]

Cyprian's eyes closed, and he moaned uncomfortably before returning to limpness. Perseus finished swathing the book and set it in the pack amidst the wheat, thinking about what Cyprian had said, not understanding it. How could providence vanish?

He gave the satyr another draught of liquid before resting again, and watching the blue sky beyond the dead tree limbs. Small patches of wispy cloud floated by. Perseus's thoughts turned to the coming night, and what they were to do until Cyprian had recovered. He thought he knew where they must go. But after Cyprian's strange words, he was uncertain.

The sun slowly passed across the sky as it had done for eons, and Perseus thought. The woods may still be full of evil. They needed shelter. But it would be horrid to sleep in a house of such evil, even if the *drakamor* was gone. At last, Perseus decided they would go to David's trailer if it were not occupied, and rest there as long as they needed.

As soon as the decision was made, Perseus put everything he had inside the pack and slung it over a shoulder. He wrapped Cyprian in the cloak and gently gathered him in his arms. Then, Perseus found the road and walked the short distance to David's trailer.

*   *   *   *

The trailer was small and rotting. And although it had a bad smell, it did not smell evil; it smelled empty. Perseus walked up the rickety stairs and called into the open doorway. After no one answered, he entered the living room; it was empty as expected, and in disarray. The yellow couch and chair were ripped, cotton stuffing pulled from their cushions and strewn about the room. The coffee table in the middle was overturned. The large black box across the room was broken; glass lay about the floor beneath it. Above the box was the only thing in the room untouched. It was a framed picture of a man whose soft brown eyes were deceptively kind, though they reminded Perseus of his own. And the man strangely reminded Perseus of himself. This picture, Perseus took from the wall and hid before doing anything else.

He turned the couch cushions over and lay Cyprian on the untouched side before straightening up the room. By the time he had finished, dusk was over the land. The room looked glum and depressing. The wind rattled the thin windows; a cold air bent through the house. Perseus sat in the chair next to Cyprian, staring out the window into the front lawn, keeping guard, sword at the ready.

He took out the horn of the river demon and set it on the coffee table, watched its surface swirl unnaturally but majestically in the darkness. Distorted images formed on the watery surface, but receded before Perseus knew what they were, if they were anything at all. Another thing to ponder.

When the moon rose, a great weariness overcame Perseus. It took him a moment to realize that the nymph's grace had left him. Exhaustion flowed through his limbs as never before, and Perseus struggled to remain awake. Somehow, he managed.

Halfway through the night Cyprian stirred restlessly. Perseus gave him a small mouthful of water, and the satyr awoke with a fright, screaming. He threw off the cloak, arms flailing wildly. Two of the deeper wounds broke open and bled.

"You're safe," Perseus said calmly, wishing to comfort Cyprian, fearing to touch him lest more wounds break open. Slowly the satyr calmed, and Perseus laid the cloak back over his body.

"Perseus?" he asked in an exhausted and confused voice.

"It is I," Perseus replied, but Cyprian had fallen asleep again.

*   *   *   *

When the first rays of light fell upon the earth, Perseus gently pulled the cloak off of Cyprian and inspected the wounds. They looked slightly better, but not much; the *drakamor's* taint had worked deeply into the young body. Perseus woke Cyprian, and gave him another mouthful of the nectar.

Seeing light and not darkness comforted him. For Cyprian calmly opened his eyes and spoke with ease, weak as he was. "I thought you dead," he said.

"As I almost was," Perseus replied. "The grace of the gods has not seen it proper to dispose of me yet. The same for you."

"Yes," Cyprian agreed. "Though I feel as if I have been drugged and beaten. I am tired and exhausted, yet when I sleep it is restless, filled with nightmares of the days past."

Perseus laughed quietly, knowing only too well how that felt. His laugh faded and he became serious. "And that may continue for a long time if we continue on the same path."

"You have the book, then," Cyprian said.

"I do."

"The same path it is then," Cyprian said.

A smile lit Perseus's lips. "Then you will have to take comfort while you can, though that will not be much. Your wounds are many and are slow to heal. Even with the help of the willow water."

"Willow water?"

"From a nymph," Perseus replied.

Cyprian's eyes grew bright, in remembrance of the nymph, then dulled again. "I thought you dead," he said again, and yawned. "You must tell me what happened."

"There is much we must catch up on, young one. But you are still weak and need rest." Perseus held out the water skin. "Drink, and then sleep. There will be plenty of time for catching up when you are healed."

Cyprian swallowed the water and sighed comfortably before closing his eyes. "Perseus," he said.

"Yes."

"Don't leave me."

"I won't," Perseus said sadly, heartbreakingly adding in thought, *unless I have to*. His duty was to the book. "I promise."

With that, Cyprian curled into the cloak, rolled so that his head nestled between the cushions and back of the couch, and fell asleep.

*   *   *   *

When the sun reached its highest point, Perseus stretched his legs for the first time. He walked into the adjoining kitchen and searched the refrigerator and cabinets. Among all sorts of strange food in weird wrappings, Perseus found the fridge full of Sprite and one of the cabinets full of Star Crunches. He sensed these were sacrifices of a sort—the kind that David's parents made, hoping that somehow they would bring their son back.

Absently, Perseus wondered about the fate of the parents—whether they had been killed, or perhaps frightened away. The more he thought about it, the more he thought they had been scared away. The woods here were quiet, and Perseus surmised that was because everything else had been scared away by the *drakamor*.

Though, once the woodland creatures learned of the evil's departure the quiet would change, and the woods would most likely fill with strangeness. Until then, Perseus would be glad for the silence.

He scooped up a box of Star Crunches and a couple cans of Sprite, and headed into the living room. He picked up a book he had found on the floor. On the front was the picture of a half-naked man and a woman dressed in a thin robe. They were lying together in a field of gold, mixed with blue and yellow flowers. The title was *Love of the Forbidden*.

*   *   *   *

Perseus watched over Cyprian day and night, also keeping watch of the woods through the dirty window above the couch. In the first two days, Cyprian woke for brief periods of time in which Perseus gave him mouthfuls of the willow water. They talked little because Cyprian was, for the most part, still in a daze. But each time Cyprian awoke he asked Perseus questions.

The first questions were difficult, and Perseus answered them by telling Cyprian the stories his mother told him when had been sick as a boy. They were stories of myth and legend, adventure and peril. Perseus's father and mother told the same story differently. Mother masking the sinister sides of the tales through her masterful recitation. Father elaborating on the demons, spirits, and gore. Perseus told the tales as his mother would, opting for the lighter version while darkness remained in Cyprian's red and puffy wounds.

Day by day, through persistent bathing in the willow water, the wounds improved, though excruciatingly slow. The long hours Cyprian had spent in the dwelling had done him ill, and occasionally black puss oozed from the gashes. But as the days passed, the puss flowed lighter.

It was the bleeding, however, that Perseus feared. The wounds bled at random. Each time he saw new blood, Perseus cringed. He wished to seek more Elderberry leaves from the forest, yet feared harm would find Cyprian if he left. So, Perseus applied fresh bandages and waited by Cyprian's side.

He remained awake around the clock, watching for the danger he sensed drawing closer, danger from the forest. But there was no choice but to wait until Cyprian's wounds were healed.

Eventually, near the beginning of the fifth day in David's trailer, the wounds stopped bleeding and began closing up. As they did so, Cyprian woke more frequently and his questions became regular. Perseus could no longer ignore them. It was nighttime on the sixth day when Cyprian awoke and again asked about the book.

"Did you find it?"

"It is safe…" Perseus answered, echoing the words that Cyprian had said days ago,…*though it is different*. In the days that had passed, Perseus often thought about Cyprian's prophetic words. *The cloth is blank…strangeness…providence has vanished*. They had passed through Perseus's mind time and time again. Could the prophecy mean that the future was empty?

The questions surrounding Cyprian's prophecy had kept Perseus occupied during the long hours of night while he watched the forest gloom. The answers might have been found inside the book itself, if Perseus dared to open it. Yet none of the answers might be there. More questions might arise. And what of the danger that followed the book? Many people had searched for the book over the millennia. Would they know it had been found? Would they remember? Those answers would surely be found on the ancient pages. But what would be unleashed if Perseus foolishly opened it, if anything?

"And what of us?" Cyprian asked. "Are we safe?"

"For now," Perseus answered, and gazed out the window.

The front yard, road, and woods beyond were lit with moonlight, and showed nothing. Indeed they were safe for the present. But Perseus felt danger blowing on the northern breeze. And with each day they remained still, Perseus's unease grew. He wished to leave this strange land and return to the land he knew. Yet Cyprian needed to rest, and to risk a journey while he was still weak was foolishness. And a journey where?

Once, two days ago, during high noon, Perseus had ventured outside the little trailer and walked to the road. He looked east. Thaeron was on the distant horizon, yet the black lights David had sought weren't there. Even if they had been, Perseus could not defy Teiresias's words. The underworld was closed to him.

"Perseus," Cyprian said. He yawned.

"Yes?"

"Tell me what happened at the bridge."

"Pray let me hold off on that story for now," he said. "I fear to tell of such things until you are fully healed."

"As you wish," Cyprian said. "Tell me another story, then. Please."

Perseus laughed softly and recalled another tale of his mother's. He began the tale of king Midas and his foolish love of gold, only to have Cyprian fall asleep within the first minute. The story trailed off and Perseus went into the kitchen. He brought back another box of Star Crunches, the third he had opened since coming to the house. He took one of the snacks, opened the wrapper, and bit into the caramel goodness.

He glanced out the window into the pale moon shadows, and for the first time saw movement. It could have been nothing more than a woodland animal returning, or it could be something worse. Either way, life was returning to the quiet reaches of the hillside. If dangerous things were not here already, they would be soon.

The next day, the seventh day since killing the *drakamor*, the sun crested the eastern mountains and shone brightly upon the small trailer. As the rays streamed through the lone window, Perseus saw that Cyprian's last wound had fully closed.

Cyprian woke sometime around mid-morning. Perseus gave him a draught of the almost depleted nymph water, and a star crunch when Cyprian asked for food. The satyr gobbled the snack, then asked for something else to eat, something less sweet. Perseus produced an apple, which Cyprian ate greedily.

"What's in that?" Cyprian asked, nodding to the pouch in Perseus's lap.

"A trophy," Perseus answered. "From the River."

"Will you tell me then what happened?" Cyprian asked.

"I have been restless for seven days, and wish a couple hours sleep," Perseus replied. "Life has sprung to your cheeks and you are in good spirits. There will be time enough for stories, I imagine. If it's okay with you, I'd like to chance a nap while you are awake."

"If that is what you wish," Cyprian said.

"You must keep watch, though, ill as you are. Life has come back to these woods, and I fear it will bring unwanted evil."

"I will keep watch," Cyprian said.

With that, Perseus lay his head on the back of the chair, propped his feet up on the coffee table, and fell asleep.

*   *   *   *

He woke to a light tapping on his shoulder. It was dark outside, and a steady rain pelted the tin roof of the trailer. Perseus was warm, and found a blanket covering his body. Cyprian sat beside him, yawning.

"I cannot stay awake any longer," Cyprian said. "I would have let you sleep the night through, but that you wished a watchman."

"You have let me sleep too long already," Perseus said. "But sleep now, and regain your strength. We must be off as soon as you are able."

In the night, Perseus saw phantoms in the rain. He never saw more than one phantom at a time, but felt that there were many. They were small, barely disturbing the rain as it fell, and looked to be a woodland creature. However, Perseus felt uneasy not knowing for sure. They made no noise and eventually there were no more to be seen. Their appearance during a rainstorm was very odd, and Perseus was on edge. He sat rigid and tense, listening for any sign of their return, seeking any sign that they knew he and Cyprian were inside. None came.

The rain subsided and morning came gray and brisk. Cyprian awoke with the light. The redness of his wounds had diminished, though it had not disappeared. Perseus gave him the last of the nymph water and then walked into the kitchen. It was time to prepare for the journey. There were foodstuffs already neatly piled on the counter.

"I see you were busy while I slept," Perseus called to the other room.

Cyprian was on his feet and in the doorway. "I felt the need to walk around," he said, "though it drained me."

"And it may still for many weeks," Perseus said. "But tomorrow we must leave. My mind has been darkening, and it is better to be on the move than stagnant. We shall take what we need from this house and set off in the morning."

Together, Perseus and Cyprian went through the house collecting food, blankets, and other things they thought they might need, including a well-made hunting knife and a pack of matches. Perseus found a small t-shirt and a pair of sweat pants in a small dresser in one of the rooms. He gave the clothes to Cyprian, who agreed to wear them only when they might meet another person from this world.

They collected the belongings into a pile in the living room. Perseus dumped out the wheat in the pack in favor of the flour he found in the kitchen. The rest of the belongings, they piled into both the pack, and a large green book bag Perseus found in the hall closet. When all the labor was done, Perseus sat in his chair and spoke.

"The path that lies before us is not clear to me," he said. "It is time I hear the parts of the tale hidden from me. And you shall hear the parts hidden from you. Then, we will decide which way our course lies."

Cyprian nodded in hesitant agreement and told his part of the tale, beginning with his chase of the bridge downstream. Then continuing along the road until he found the crucifix and into the woods with the blood vines. He reluctantly told of coming to the *drakamor* house and entering the dark expanse, and of his vision of Perseus. His tale ended with the first account of whirring air; the rest was forgotten or lost in memory, and that's the way Cyprian preferred it; much pain revolved around what he remembered.

Then Perseus told of his story from beginning to end—waking up in the oracle's care, and what he remembered of those days that seemed forever ago. He dwelled on the oracle's tale of the book and the priest who stole it, remembering Sara's caution about the priest living outside the book's pages; that dark unknown troubled Perseus deeply. He then glazed over the times that he and Cyprian were together, but recounted them all the same so that the entire tale was told, finally coming to his encounter with the river demon...

* * * *

"...the river's rage was fierce and pulled the bridge from its foundation as I stood in the middle. It was not despair that filled me, but joy. It had been a long time since my sword spilled blood. The bridge spilt in two, witness to the power of the demon. Dark water swirled behind me, sought to grab my ankle and drag me into its depths. The demon loosed the bridge's grip from the shore and sank beneath the waves. Into the water the bridge sank, I its only passenger.

Water rushed upward as the bridge broke apart, and my joy lessened as a strong arm pulled me under the water. I was freed with a slash of my sword, but the river came on stronger, grabbed my wrist, and held on with a ferocity beyond the thunder-striker himself.

We joined in battle, foot locked with foot, fingers with fingers, brow to brow, resolving never to yield an inch. Splinters and branches pelted my body and eyes, yet I did not falter. Three times I pressed, struggling to break the demon's lock without success. The fourth time, however, his hands came unfastened. I struck him with my fist and whirled around him, clung to his back, crushing him in my iron grip.

Outmatched and out-manned, he used the art of his and disappeared, dissolved into nothing, and I was left grappling with the water alone. A second later, his mighty grip was locked around my throat from behind; my luck turned in an instant. Fire pierced my lungs and throat; my windpipe was in a vice, I in agony. I fought to free my gullet from his thumbs, and on the verge of breaking his grip, the demon once again dissolved.

I laughed as I might, knowing he was breathless, and I still with strength, as little as it was, to charge forth if my foe should show himself once more. I searched the dirty water tirelessly. Harsh bits of sand, stone, and wood came at me from the swirling darkness, cutting my tender skin. Without finding the demon, I resolved to head for the surface and breathe of the fresh air again.

As I neared the hazy light, my foot caught on nothing, and slowly I was dragged downward. My breath was almost out, yet I drew upon the last reserve and turned to face the river. His mighty arms clung to my body, and indeed it seemed I was being crushed by a mountain. Even so, I managed to insert my sweating arms between his and dislodge his grip. I spun and caught his strong, stiff horn in my fist. The demon dove deeper, and I found myself upon the bottom of the river, struggling to gain footing in the soft mud. I clung to the horn with all my might as the sprite spun and twirled, trying to evade my grasp.

Finally, my feet found ground. I planted myself and took hold of the other horn. The sprite disappeared before my eyes, yet his horns remained in my grasp. With a mighty tug, I wrenched them apart.

A great bellow shook the river's bottom, and my foe was vanquished. Good for me, cause darkness was clouding my thoughts. The destruction of my enemy had almost destroyed me as well. I struck out for the wide sky above and swam forever through darkness, finally entering the realm of hazy light. My breath gave out before I reached the surface, and water filled my lungs. Still, I swam, fighting death the entire way, and found air, though it was difficult to breathe. I crawled onto the shore and collapsed..."

✳   ✳   ✳   ✳

Perseus continued the tale with his short time with the nymph and traveling untouched through the wood, passing the one house that was still awake. He dwelled on that house, telling every detail—the blue siding, the brown shutters, and the orange light that proclaimed it the house of a soothsayer. It was this house that Perseus wanted to travel to, to seek knowledge about their path. But he told of his doubts about the seer, speaking the strange prophecy Cyprian had given but did not remember...*the clooth is blank*...leaving Cyprian dumbstruck. Perseus then finished with his part, coming to the crucifix, entering the house, defeating the *drakamor,* and finally, tending and watching over Cyprian.

When all was said, it was nearly dark again, and the trailer was silent as Perseus and Cyprian thought to themselves. They took a quiet dinner of apples and sweet peaches that came from a can.

Clouds hid the stars, and it was difficult to see any difference between lawn and forest through the window. Although they had found candles while searching the trailer, they did not light them for fear of what they would attract. It was gloomy in the dark silence.

At last Cyprian spoke.

"I can think of no better course than to seek the seer," he said quietly, hiding his disappointment that this was not the end of the quest, "though I feel our path lies forward and not back. It is such a small distance to travel there is no reason not to seek council, as doubtful as it may be."

"It is settled then," Perseus said. "We leave tomorrow, mid-morning. There is one errand that must be done at first light."

They spent the next hour packing up their new supplies. Perseus took first watch, using his time to fashion a new cloak from a woolen blankets. Early in the second hour of his watch a chittering sound echoed throughout the woods. Perseus sat up straight, searching the darkness.

Small shadows, many shadows covered the front lawn, bringing the chittering with them. They walked across the lawn, disappearing and emerging from the woods on either side. The chittering shadows surrounded the house, waking Cyprian with a fright. Perseus laid a hand on his chest and put a hushed finger to his mouth, and the two sat quietly, not daring to make any noise.

At last, the chittering grew soft and finally quit, leaving an intense silence.

"What was that?" Cyprian finally asked.

"I do not know," Perseus replied. "But I am glad we are staying here no longer."

Cyprian nodded. "I shan't be able to sleep for a while. I'll take watch?"

"So be it," Perseus said, and lay his head down on the backrest.

They switched watches until the light of morning. Perseus charged Cyprian to look over the packs and make sure everything was in order, while he ran his errand. He took two sheets from a back bedroom, walked through the front door, and down the rickety stairs. On the ground were tiny animal prints, embedded in the soft soil. Five long, skinny toes poked out from the each sole. Though their massed tread was confusion, it was clear they were four legged creatures.

After inspecting the prints for all the information they would give, which was almost none, Perseus turned to the woods and walked downhill. In less than a minute he came to the dead clearing and the now dull house contained within.

He walked onto the porch and hesitated at the open doorway. It was not black. Only the empty entryway and the hallway beyond looked out at Perseus. The *drakamor* was gone, of that Perseus was sure, yet the house felt evil. Though the feel caused Perseus to pause at the doorway, it made him sure of his errand.

He entered and stood in the entryway. He meant to head straight for the room on his left, but he was drawn forward into the hallway. Just beyond the light of the doorway, couched in the shadows and debris, was the crucifix. It was charred a golden black and it held Perseus's gaze for a moment. He picked it up and stuffed it behind his belt.

Then he turned and began his errand. He entered the room where he had found the book, and where David and Billy's remains still lay. He stretched the sheets on top of each other on the floor and carefully laid the remains of the boys in them, before wrapping them up tightly and carrying them out into the open.

$$*\qquad*\qquad*\qquad*$$

Back at David's house, Perseus laid the bundled bones upon the small bed in the back room and said a prayer. He would have liked to give them a proper funeral, raising a pyre in their name and giving sacrifice in their honour, but time was short and a fire would draw unwanted attention. He returned outside and gathered six handfuls of dirt in a small blanket. The dirt he spread on top of the boy's bones—an adequate burial for the circumstances—before adding packages of Star Crunches and a few cans of Sprite.

He then forced Cyprian to put on the sweat pants and the small t-shirt. To the road and down the hill they went until they came upon the Fairfield Road. Down that road they tread to the house of the soothsayer. The house was dark. The orange light no longer glowed, but remained a cold outline in the window. The blinds were drawn shut and the space behind them seemed devoid of life.

Perseus covered his sword with his cloak before banging on the front door. There was no answer. He banged again. Silence. He again set his mighty fist on the thin wood, and only after a minute could he hear sound from inside.

"Coming," a voice grumbled angrily, and then mumbled lowly. "Stupid bastards."

Seconds later there were several loud clicks as the locks were being undone. The door opened, and framed in it was a middle-aged woman. Her hair had been black, but was turning gray. The entire mess was frizzled and hung well below her shoulders. Her face was pale, the skin drooping from her cheeks, wrinkles lining her eyes. She was dressed in a pale blue robe that was open, revealing a long white nightgown. Her feet were bare. She cradled a rifle in her right arm; the index finger of her left hand rested on the trigger.

"Who are you?" she demanded, lips curled into annoyance.

Although Perseus did not know exactly what the object in the woman's arms was, he understood it was dangerous. He kept his voice calm and even as he spoke.

"We seek the wisdom of a seer," he said to the woman.

"I ain't no seer," the woman grumbled, and pointed toward the window with the unlit sign. "Cain't you read? Psy—Chic. Psychic."

"I apologize," Perseus said, as nice as he could muster. "We have come to take council."

The woman's face lost a hint of its annoyance. "If you want your fortune read, you'll have to make an appointment," she mumbled, and then muttered under her breath. "Seems everyone's wanting their fortune read of late." Again she spoke aloud. "I'm booked for the next two weeks. Call back after seven in the evening, before eight, and I'll put you in sometime after the 20th."

The woman stepped back and swung the door in Perseus's face. He placed a foot inside the door before it shut. "We are in a great hurry," he called as the door rebounded open. The woman stood back from the door, holding the rifle straight out, aimed directly at Perseus's chest.

"Get away," she said. "Get away now, and don't come back."

There was anger in her voice, but fear as well. Perseus remained where he was. The woman shook the gun at him and screamed for him to get away. When he did not move she walked forward, shaking the gun, threatening.

When she had come close enough, Perseus made his move. Lightning fast he threw aside his cloak, drew his sword, and swung, hitting the barrel of the gun with the flat side of the sword. At the same time the gun flew from the woman's hands, a loud blast filled the small entryway. Plaster fell from the ceiling and the gun hit the wall and clattered to the floor. Smoke exited the barrel is small tendrils, quickly wafting away.

The woman's face melted into fear as Perseus entered the house. She staggered into the light green wall behind her and sunk to the floor. "Don't hurt me," she pled.

As Perseus calmly put his sword back in his belt, he glanced at a stack of newspapers next to the door. The words of the article caught his attention...*them woods...darker...trees looked different...*"That is the last thing on my mind," he said, tearing his eyes away from the article. "We need your council for our journey and that is all. But we need it now."

He held his hand out for the woman, who looked at him and the hand for a good while before she finally took it and allowed Perseus to help her up. The woman eyed Cyprian curiously, as he shuffled through the door.

"Very well," she finally said, scowling, unafraid anymore. "But you better pay well," she added and nodded at the bullet hole in the ceiling. "I'll need to get that fixed." She turned abruptly and walked down a small hallway.

"If your worth paying, you shall be rewarded," Perseus said dryly, following.

Without turning, the woman pointed to a room on her left that was doorless; a thick burgundy cloth hung in its stead. "Wait in there," she said, and continued down the hallway.

Perseus and Cyprian entered the dark, windowless room and through the light in the hallway saw a table in the center, surrounded by a few chairs. There were also chairs along the walls, and in these Perseus and Cyprian took their seat.

It was a long time before the woman returned. "You could have turned on the lights," she said, and flicked a switch on the wall.

Four lamps lit up around the room, casting a light glow over the space. The walls were a deep rich red and had dark flowers attached by vines painted up and down. The ceiling was olive green and in the center, over the table, was a chandelier with unlit candles. The table was round and covered with an intricately woven cloth, which was deep blue. Many stars adorned its borders. Around the edge of the cloth were golden tassels. Near the center of the table, but slightly to the side was a round ball of glass set upon a circular ring of brass. Seven chairs surrounded the table, and were made from a richly grained wood. They had high backs and plush cushions.

The woman was now garbed in a light, olive green skirt that flowed to the ground, a dark burgundy shirt that buttoned up the front, and a vest of satiny blue material covered with strange symbols and markings. Upon her head was a black turban of sorts. The woman's graying hair streamed out from underneath the turban on either side. Her face was painted with rich colors, red on her cheeks, blue on her eyes, black on her eyelashes; a vast contrast to the pale face they had seen at the door.

"Sit here," the woman said, beckoning to two chairs opposite the table from herself. When Perseus and Cyprian had taken their seats, the woman sat herself and pulled the crystal ball closer.

"Strange times are upon us," she began, waving her hands over the crystal ball. She looked from Cyprian to Perseus, gazing into their eyes with clear intent. "Evil roams the woods freely, creatures of the night come out in the day, creatures of the day fall into night. Stone turns to earth and wind carries on it tidings of sorrow. It is nothing more than change so I say, and change will come as it will."

The woman looked into the crystal ball, her expressions changing minutely as her head shifted for a better view.

"You have come from afar, I can see," she said. "But I can feel it in your soul as well. Death clings to you and will not let go. This should not be, and I fear there will be great suffering as consequence. Yet you live to a greater purpose. Choose carefully your path or else fail."

The woman looked up from the crystal ball and fell silent.

"Is that all?" Perseus asked.

The woman nodded. "Your future is clouded in the ball," she said. "Especially at ten in the morning!"

"You have told us nothing that we have not seen firsthand," Perseus said. "That you yourself have seen out your front window. There is no foresight in your words, and you deserve nothing for your troubles." Perseus stood, and motioned Cyprian to do the same. "Let us not waste any more time."

"I said your future is clouded in the ball," the woman said quickly. "Come, sit down. Let me consult the stars. What is your sign?"

"The stars," Perseus said absently, sitting back down. The Great Hunter. He had forgotten about his conversation with the oracles.

Deliver the book from harm and those who would seek it. Hide it. Fail, and the world will unravel...

But how? You have said nothing of how.

We know not where your path lies after you retrieve the book...There was one vision, and one alone...though it answers no questions...of the Great Hunter...all I can give you for council.

"What's your sign," the woman repeated.

"Sign," Perseus mouthed.

"Your zodiac sign. What month were you born in?"

"I don't know," Perseus said. The woman knew nothing...*the clooth is blank*...if she ever did...*previdence has vanished*...It was the Great Hunter that would guide their future, though what that meant was hidden from Perseus. "Cyprian, we are done here. This woman knows nothing. Let's go."

"Nothing," the woman scoffed. "Ha! I've given you a reading as fine as you'll find."

"That I believe," Persues replied. "But a pig could have told us the same. When you have given us information we did not already know, you shall get your pay. And that might be soon." He turned to Cyprian. "We must return to our world...to follow a new path forged from the past."

"The past," Cyprian repeated quietly. "But how will we return to our world?"

"Come with me," Perseus said, and led the way out of the room to the front door. Cyprian and the woman followed. Perseus pointed down at the article on the front page. "There is another rift between worlds."

Cyprian stared at the article, reading the short blip on the front page.

Three Boys Missing In NC. —
BY DAVID MESSNER
Times Staff Writer

The disappearance of three recent high school graduates has authorities looking Northward for answers. The boys left on an extended hiking trip in the Nantahala National forest on Saturday, June 10th, and vanished. Forest rangers and volunteer firemen followed the boy's route until they came upon "spooks" in the woods, said volunteer fireman John Gayhart. "Something changed in them woods.

It became darker. And the trees looked different. And the trail that was once there disappeared."
The search team felt an overwhelming unease, and halted their progress to report the disturbance in the woods. When the authorities heard of the peculiarity of the situation, they called Fairfield in search of answers to our local disturbance.

(Cont. Pg. 9)

Cyprian stopped reading and muttering under his breath. He turned to Perseus. "What of our path in the other world?" he asked.

"That is a long story that we will have much time for," Perseus said. "And I would like to think on it for a few day to organize what I am to tell. For now, there is information we need to get back to our world." Perseus turned to the woman. "It is time for you to earn your pay."

"Wanting to talk now are you?" she said pompously, then muttered under her breath. "Probably stiff me then too."

"One gold piece for your information. Take it, or take nothing. We will get the information either way."

"Gold," she muttered silently. "Everyone wanting to pay with strange money…" Her words died out. "Gold. And you leave straight away."

"Done." Perseus said.

"What is it you are wanting to know?" the woman asked.

*   *   *   *

Less than an hour later, Perseus and Cyprian were walking through the forest, headed west, toward an old pathway that led southward to the mountains they sought. The pathway would give them seclusion from this world—a world Perseus distrusted—and would give them time to talk and think.

Late in the afternoon, after traveling across glens, hills and pastures, the landscape faded from brilliance. The air was less crisp, the wind less lofty, the earth less fertile. They had passed away from the hybrid world, headed for North Carolina and another hybrid world.

Perseus and Cyprian made camp among a patch of evergreen trees early in the afternoon, for Cyprian was still weak. After dinner and just before dusk the clouds broke up and sun shone on the earth. And though the feeling of danger had passed when they left the hybrid world behind, they set a watch and built no fire.

Perseus took first watch and studied his trophy horn. Starlight covered its swirling surface, and the crooked images again formed. Perseus turned the horn around, examining its smoothness and delicate strength, marveling at its hardness. It was powerful and would serve him well indeed. But to what purpose?

Setting the horn back in its pouch Perseus lay back and looked up at the vast sky, and for the first time since he could remember enjoyed the twinkling stars. Off to the south, looming above the horizon, he could see parts of the Great Hunter through the pine branches.

When they hit the old pathway, they would be headed south. They would be following The Great Hunter in his immortal death, something Perseus had not expected, but which struck him as the only way it could have been. When they returned to their world, though, Perseus and Cyprian would follow The Great Hunter's quest in life, or so Perseus had begun to believe. But he was unsure. And what of the book...where was it to go?

For two days, as they traveled lightly and slept heavily in the thick of forest, Perseus thought and organized the tale, which seemed to grow a difficult task as the days passed. Something had changed, though Perseus could not understand what. At night, if he could, Perseus would take his watch where he could see the constellation of Orion through the branches of fir and pine, and muse over his clouded memory.

On the third day of their journey from Donaldson Hill, Perseus and Cyprian came to the base of a long mountain chain that extended as far as they could see.

They hiked up the tree and brush littered slope to the top, and came upon a rocky pathway that meandered through the trees, heading both north and south along the mountain ridgeline. Perseus could see two rectangular, white blazes that were smaller than his hand on the trees, and was relieved that the psychic had told him the truth.

"We're here," Perseus said unenthusiastically. For the journey had just begun. It would take just under two months to hike to Nantahala. Perseus sat down on a rock, massaged his feet, and he and Cyprian took a small meal. Then, they continued southward.

That evening, Perseus called a stop to the hiking in the early evening as usual. In the three days since leaving Donaldson Hill, Cyprian had almost fully recovered his strength. He had rationed the remainder of the nymph water, taking a small mouthful each night, relishing the cool comfort that came with the draught, wishing it to last forever. Tonight, however, when he retrieved the skin from his pack, he found it empty.

"That's right..." he muttered sadly as he put the skin down. He had finished the last of the water the previous night.

After they made camp and had eaten dinner, Perseus led Cyprian through the woods toward an opening in the trees. "It is time to begin the story of Orion," he said as they walked. "At least what I remember of it. Something is clouding my memory."

The clearing turned out to be a rock outcropping slightly off the ridge. The landscape was dotted with lights and a brisk, but warm breeze blew up the rock face. Perseus directed Cyprian's attention to the southern sky, toward where the constellation of Orion lay above the horizon. It was the first unobstructed view of the stars he had had since waking in the oracle's cottage. Then, something had been wrong with the Jewel star. And though Perseus remembered that much, the queerness then had not caused him alarm. But what he saw now caused him deep alarm. The Jewel star was gone.

"It's missing," Perseus said, and saw that Cyprian was confused. He pointed to the constellation. "The Jewel star. There were three stars in the hunter's belt. Now there are only two, the middle one gone."

Perseus forced his eyes away from the constellation. It was not right to look so. The stars were supposed to be immortal, and yet they were changing as all else was. The underworld was unbinding. The mortal world was entering into chaos. Two worlds were melding. The words in the book of Antioch had not just been changed, they had disappeared. What was happening?

Questions upon questions bombarded Perseus as he stood on the rock outcrop. He controlled their flow by leading Cyprian away from the rocks, out of sight of the stars, and back to camp. He silently gathered wood and built a fire. As he and Cyprian sat by the soft glow, Perseus tried to remember the beginning of the tale of Orion, but it would not come. He could only think of the Jewel star and the underworld and the raiders in Delphi. And as he thought, everything led to the oracles. They were the end to one life and the beginning to a new. And it was with thinking of the oracles that Perseus finally found words.

"The oracles had a vision, Cyprian. A vision of The Great Hunter. But it was dim and meant nothing to them. As it means nothing to me now. Or at least its meaning is hidden. If only I had remembered earlier…" he paused. What had happened had happened, and nothing could change it. The only thing to do was to look forward. "It is Orion's path I thought we must follow," Perseus resumed, "though now I doubt everything I once knew. Everything changed since the lights appeared in the meadow cottage. For you and I both. And for that, whatever decision is made, must be made by both of us. Do you agree that we must return to our world?

"Yes," Cyprian answered and yawned, suddenly struck by a great mount of tiredness. "Yes."

"Then we shall continue southward toward Nantahala," Perseus continued. "After that, there is nothing known. I am no longer sure we will follow Orion's deeds, for I no longer trust that I know them. But I will tell what I remember."

Perseus poked the fire. He remained silent and pushed the coals around, trying to remember the beginning. It had something to do with Aegyptus. No, not Aegyptus. Boetia. Boetia was the beginning. Orion was born from Boetia. But how? And why. There had been a drought. Yes, that was right. A great drought that lasted seven years. And a man named Hyreius. That was where the tale began.

"The tale," Perseus finally said, "begins in the ages before the ages…"

END OF BOOK I

Author's Note

Everything is nothing,
And nothing is what is seems,
You may know what it says,
But how bout what it means,
The answer lies part in thought,
And partly in the seams,
Nothing is everything,
And everything is what it seems.

Book II *Tales of the Lyre* is on its way. Look for bigger and better things.

Many thanks to many people…you know who you are. I'll say no more.

Contact: adamhoch@providencevanished.com

Distributors: Ingram and Baker & Taylor

Website: www.providencevanished.com

Endnotes

1. Awakenings

2. Madam. You and yours have done me a kind service. I am blessed by your sanctity and grace, and will pay you for the compassion however I might.

3. But you are an oracle.

4. Beware, young sir.

5. Unwanted Memories

6. You'll be sorry if you don't stop.

7. Taenarus

8. I descended through Taenarus's gate, in search of Hades dark and great. Through the throngs of wraiths and spirits I went, more grieved than a doves spent cry; not in search of the underworld, but to speak with pale Persephone, and also her husband the lord of the death, who commands the unlovely realm's heath.

9. When I came upon the lord and his queen, I prayed their memory of love sharp. 'You too were joined in love,' I said, 'if the old tales are not false. By this kingdom filled with fear and grace, these infinite quiet realms, an honourable place, restore, I ask, I implore, I beg of thee, the fate yielded to my Eurydice.

10. To you is owed ourselves and the land, for all people living there, I have found linger a short time in conscience pity; then we hasten, quick or soon, to one dark house; here one way leads us all in time; here in the end all the worldly bells chime; over mankind you keep the longest hold. She too, when ripe years have finally grow cold, shall fall and find your palace from above. The thing I ask is to have her love; once more in my arms so

bright, the wound of loss is above my might; if the mighty fates will not pardon her, I forsake life—may two deaths give you cheer.

11. Next to the bright light, I lost my honourable strength, with joy so near, at a short length; my eye wandered through longing lust, damning my Eurydice back to darkness; she fell immediately to the house of ghosts, where I was refused a second entrance.

12. Beneath the World

13. A Tower Sight

14.

> *The mark of life is but a small part*
> *To fight the black of the drakamor heart*
> *You must know of sorrow and also of death*
> *And breathe the wickedness of evil's foul breath*
> *Before you seek the great spirit of olde*
> *Else your lifeblood will meet the ground cold*
> *And without your soul enter Hades dark door*
> *To know of tyme never more*
> *But from death's grace come their life divine*
> *Soft and small the life grows when it shines*
> *Tear the power from the deadly temple white*
> *White falls to black and has no more bite*
> *And evil cunning falls into shapeless husks*

15. Parting

16. Troubled Dreams

17. An Old Rhyme

18. Thank you, my lady. Certainly, I shall remember you best of all.

19. A New Beginning

20. Golden chance.

21. The book is safe. Though it is different, disordered, and also strange. The future has vanished; the cloth is blank. The unknown is all that is certain.

0-595-32729-X

Printed in the United States
21822LVS00004BC/88-228